The item should be returned or renewed by the last date stamped below.

Dylid dychwelyd neu adnewyddu'r eitem erbyn y dyddiad olaf sydd wedi'i stampio isod.

Newport Library and Information Service

To renew visit / Adnewyddwch ar
www.newport.gov.uk/libraries

Dedicated to: -

The woman who knitted Pablo Escobar's sweaters...

Other titles by Anthony Bunko

"Never trust anyone with seven toes on each foot"

Madhatma Gandhi 1908

Black Jacks

Chapters: -

Wellies in Minehead

This book is based on the hit, comedy stage play, the Wizard of Gurnwah, which has performed to sell out audiences all over the world. Well, to some of the world anyway. Also, if you look closely there are small traces of a film which I saw when I was about 8 years of age while high on life and even higher on some kind of sherbet and jelly baby cocktail. I can't remember the name of the movie but it had a lion in it, a tiger and lots of angry beaver!

biscuits

Foreword

By

Neil Maidman

(Director of The Wizard of Gurnwah)

It was late, I was up late...the world was sleeping and I was riding with the devil and carrying out the most heinous of crimes. I was checking Facebook at 130am. A notification from Alan O'Keefe pinged up on my screen. My oldest school friend. Known him forever – well, since we were 4. A cheeky little chappy who had an amazing stash of memorabilia and priceless stuff from when we were kids – Corona bottles, 30-year-old packets of long forgotten crisps and more Chopper bikes than we knew what to do with. I loved chatting online with Alan, and so when the notification came up say 'Bunko, Neil Maidman is your man. He'll direct your play for you', I felt compelled to read on. *"A 50 something bloke from Merthyr, never written a play before seeks director for his first effort of a work for the stage, based on the Wizard of Oz...set in Merthyr with weird characters and stuff."* It sounded shit...really shit, the kind of shit that smelled pretty rank too. However, I was intrigued. For two reasons, really. Firstly, I loved the name of the play – 'The Wizard of Gurnwah' and, more importantly I thought that it would allow me to bring a bit of theatre to my hometown. Something that I had never done before – in 30 years a performer and director.

I was emailed the script. Thought it too long but really funny (though I only read the Act 1)...and then I met Bunko, in what turned out to be Gurnwah Central.....'Spoons in Merthyr, one damp January night. I was early, he was late...we sat, we talked and he asked me two questions. Two very important questions....*'Is it funny or what?'* and *'Are we doing this or what?'* With a deep breath and some trepidation, I agreed and was almost immediately introduced to the warped mind of Anthony

Bunko. We met some amazing characters and some excellent local talent on that first show...and the rest is history as they say. We forge forward to this day, making people laugh in our home town. It's still all bonkers but in a good way. It's also less shit too. He has promised to take our plays all the way to Broadway...am not sure if he specified New York or that long road between Pontypridd and Treforest...knowing Bunko though, as he has done with this book, we will meet or create some characters, fun and laughter on the way. Enjoy this book...I feel as if I have lived it already before a word was written. Bunko is pure class....and his books are pretty good too. Neil xx

Thanks Alan O Keefe, for bringing us together. You were and always will be the greatest of mates. You were our biggest fan and we both miss you and hope that we do your memory proud with each laugh that we have, on the road to the GurnOz...

The bit before the book starts properly: -

Imagine a village so scary, so terrifying, and so shocking that even Fred and Rosie West in their murderous prime wouldn't dare drive through it. A place where Leatherface from the movie, *The Texas Chain Saw Massacre*, is not only the Village post man but when he attended primary school he got voted the pretty boy most likely to succeed in the outside world. A place so behind the times that they have never seen a mobile phone or Sky TV and have never tasted the delights of McDonald's chicken nuggets. A place where wild animals freely roam about and sheep look worried (and not because of the wild animals). A place where...ok, ok...enough, enough...I could go on like this until the two-headed cows come home.

You get the picture by now!

The aim of this 'educational' manuscript is simple. Its objective is to unlock the door with the key to your dark and warped imagination. Beyond it lies another dimension; a dimension of sound, a dimension of sight, a dimension of mind. You will move into a land of both shadows and substance, of things and ideas, of sheep and banjos and real dull fuckers...So strap yourself in...because you've just crossed over into......the....

(quick turn over the page...)

Bedlinog-zone

This is where the story, my friends, based on a few true events and a bucket full of made-up shit, slowly expands across each page like someone spreading real butter on thick, white, toasted bread.

Chapter 1

THERE'S NO PLACE LIKE...

Terry the dog sat cross-legged on a large rock next to a fast-flowing stream. In his paws, he embraced an old banjo like a long-lost lover from Liverpool. *(I know, I know, what you are thinking. This story already sounds unbelievable. However, what you need to remember is, if life is a box of chocolates, then this novel is more like a slightly burnt, out-of-date Fray Bentos chicken and mushroom pie. It looks good, smells lovely but is usually full of weird tasting stuff. So, eat away!)*

For where he lived, Terry the dog was an unusually handsome, cute, brown and white mutt with a sharp sense of mischief and an enormous appetite for humping anything that moved. Like most of the dogs in the village, he was your typical Heniz 57 variety kinda mongrel. Apparently, the dog's mother, Mary Jane, the bitch, was well known for loving a bit of the old, red lipstick.

'She's had more cocks in her short life than tins of Pedigree Chum,' her owner bragged to the cast of drunks in the Rugby club on a Sunday morning.

This honest confession about his dog wasn't lost on the pack of old, grey-haired committeemen. That afternoon, an emergency meeting was organised. The outcome was Mary Jane, the bitch, became the rugby club's mascot...or the club's concubine...or concub-mutt!

Deep down, Terry hoped his dad was the big, black mastiff that lived at the top of the village with the bloke everyone called Reservoir Head because of being born with a severe case of water on the brain. But if the truth be known, Terry's dad could have been any of the few dozen wild dogs that roamed the village. He could even have been the seed from the loins of several amorous chickens, or Desmond the devil goat who had a bent penis with a bell-end shaped like Alan Shearer's head. Alas, Terry would never know who his real biological father was, but there were whispers the mutt did have the exact same ears as a certain Bernie the Secretary of the rugby club who used to walk the club mascot up into the woods several times a week, and twice on Sundays. (Enough said!!)

Anyway, that's enough of Terry and his search to find his fur and blood, let's continue with our story.

As the darkened rain clouds clambered over the mountaintops to cover the lifeless valley in an eerie afternoon twilight, Terry sat strumming his banjo. 'Brrrrrringggggg,' the perfectly pitched chord rose into the afternoon skies.

From high up on the old, rickety bridge, which straddled the cloudy stream, a weird looking boy in tattered clothes and a mono-brow that the Gallagher brothers in their *"Definitely Maybe"* period would have died for, strummed out the same chord on a homemade guitar made from a Cuban cigar box and some elastic bands. *(I know, I know...but don't forget, this is Fray Bentos pie time, not Cadbury orange creams.)*

'Brrrriiiiiingggg...Brrrriiiiiingggg,' the weird boy strummed.

With a grin on its face, Terry the dog looked up. The boy on the bridge beamed back, revealing a mouth full of teeth so rotten, they looked like he had sellotaped a bunch of raw broccoli to his tongue.

'So, it's a dual you be a-wantin',' Terry barked.

'Yeeeeepppp,' came back the reply.

Terry the dog knew the weird boy could play. Even with webbed fingers and eyes so crossed his black pupils nearly touched in the middle, the boy had proved many times over, he was a master when it came to jamming on the old cigar box guitar. Many called him the bonky-eyed Jimi Hendrix of the cowshed. Nevertheless, Terry the dog was more than confident in his own ability. The talented mongrel was more than happy to accept the challenge laid down by the weird looking youth with the awful green teeth.

With a quick nod of the head towards each other, the duelling banjo contest began. Or, the duelling dog banjo and Cuban cigar box guitar contest if we were being more precise, began. Back and forth the musical battle commenced. Terry the dog blasting out a few bars, followed note for note by the creepy boy on the bridge. Their playing got more passionate and more complicated with each byzantine movement of their hands, or in Terry's case, with each byzantine movement of his paw.

(NB – if you don't know what byzantine means, you dull twat, then ask your defence lawyer!)

A big, brown bear hunting for food in the nearby stream, plucked up its ears to listen to the music. *(No, it didn't do a little jig. Now that would be stupid. If you must know, the creature just stood there, clicking its fingers like the Jazzy bloke off the Fast Show.)*

All of a sudden, from out of an outhouse, appeared a thick-set human with a long, jet black beard like the bloke from ZZ Top. The person's dirty dungarees hung down around his ankles. A sheep, with an expression on its face as if it had eaten three, extra strong mints on a cold day on top of Pen-y-fan mountain, sat positioned comfortably between the individual's legs. *(Just as a little side note, the sheep wore knee length, schoolgirl, white pop socks and had an Alice band in its hair. Don't ask!)*

'Ooooo, look Doris,' the person in the filthy jeans oooo'd, 'it's a feckin' barn dance.' The human being and the animal jigged along to the music while grinding their groins together like a slutty couple from the BBC hit show, *Strictly Cum Dogging*.

The music continued. The odd-looking individual jigged and danced near the mineshaft. With its eye's tightly shut, the sheep laid back and thought of England, or probably, Wales!

In the background, with a rumbling belly and 4 pups to feed back at bear camp, the big, brown bear soon got bored and went back to chasing malformed fish swimming in the shallow waters.

Just then, a loud screeching sound brought everything back to normality. 'Terry,' a girl's voice rang out from somewhere behind a line of half-dead trees.

The dog and weird boy were too engrossed in their battle to hear it.

'Terry...Terry,' the girl appeared like a ray of light out of the darkness in her blue and white checked summer dress. In her hand, a bucket full to the brim with freshly picked goosegogs.

Luckily for Terry, he spied the girl just before she noticed him. In a panic, he chucked his banjo into a clump of weeds and did what dogs normally did in situations like this. He lay back on the grass, lifted his right leg and began licking his balls as if he was licking gravy off a large oval plate served up in the best carvery in the Valleys.

'Terry...what have I told you about playing with that Dozy Git,' Dorothy looked at her pet. The mutt looked at his old boy. 'No...not that thing,' she pointed to the weird boy heading towards them. 'Him!'

Leaping over a tree stump, the weird boy spat on his hand. He used the gob to flatten down his matted hair. 'Don't be like that Doroffffeeeeeeeey,' the odd-looking youth spoke with a lisp,' 'youuuuuss will be Misses Dozy Git one day.'

Dorothy made a face as if she was sucking half a lemon while she had a large, open boil on her tongue. 'Now, now Dozy...I can't marry you...you're my first cousin.'

Tears filled his bonky eyes.

The person in the dungarees sidled up beside her. 'What about marrying me then, Dorothy?' the mumbled words escaped from the person's mouth like an overweight husband in a gravy stained white vest holding a conversation with his long-suffering wife while chewing on a tough leg of lamb.

'Certainly not,' replied the pretty looking girl.

'Oh, here's she goes again. Miss Bloody Picture-Perfect,' the individual hissed.

Dorothy let go of a loud sigh. 'Not this again,' she muttered, 'it's always Miss Bloody Picture-Perfect. I'm bleedin' sick of it.'

'But it is true...just look at you. Who the hell do you think you are?'

Dorothy sighed. Being known as 'Miss Bloody Picture-Perfect' had always been a giant anchor tied around her perfectly formed neck. In the cold light of day, this was Bedlinog not some Walt Disney movie. Having a full set of nice, straight, white teeth, four normal fingers and a thumb on each of her two hands, without a hint of webbing, had sentenced the poor girl to a lifetime of being called a 'freak' in the village of Bedlinog.

It all began, a few minutes before she got born. In the drizzling rain, outside the cow shed, which often doubled up as the village hospital, the both families of Dorothy's parents waited impatiently like the cast of the Adams family eyeballing the Munsters at the Elvis Presley festival down Porthcawl. Underneath the big conker tree, a half-dead ceremonial pig roasted slowly on a spit over a roaring fire. The family members chanted loudly as they all waited for the sprog to emerge and the wild celebrations to commence.

In spite of all the anticipation building up outside the shed, inside things suddenly went from bad to....to...damn-right bizarre when the new-born finally popped out.

'How many toes have she got?' Dorothy's father asked, puffing his chest out with pride. Deep down he hoped the nurse would mutter. 'She's got three big, fat ones,' or maybe 'eight,' or better still, 'she's got one huge crab claw like your Uncle Cyril?' His smile lit up with excitement over the possible answer.

However, his simple question was met with a deafening silence. The nurse struggled to reply. '5,' she eventually muttered, 'the girl's got 5.'

'5! Are you sure?' he muttered. The nurse nodded.

'Oh ok...but how webbed are they?' piped up the mother, 'I hope they are like my Cousin Alison's. Did you know her fingers and feet were so webbed, that when David Attenborough made a documentary about the village in the early 70's, he was convinced she was three-quarter toad?' she added with a certain smugness.

This time the nurse shook her head. The big wart on her cheek wobbled like blackcurrant jelly on a plate. 'I'm afraid they're not webbed. In fact, she's got nothing wrong with her at all. No bonky eye, no cleft palate, no lizard shaped tongue and not a hunchback in sight.' She took a deep breath, 'she hasn't even got horns or fangs.' The nurse spat on the floor, 'She's very strange looking. She looks just like the girl in that terrible, scary movie we saw once in the club house. What was her name again?'

'Regan from the Exorcist?' the mother beamed, 'I loved that film. I hope she looks like her...but after she got possessed of course. Such a lovely, ugly bitch.'

'No...not that film. The one with the little men in it.'

'Alien?' the father yelled. 'Yes...she's all green and slimy...perfect...just perfect.' He did a little dance to celebrate. It was short lived.

'No,' the nurse muttered, 'not alien...that real horrible film, you know...Snow fuckin' White.'

The shocked parents stared at each other. In a shaky voice, the distraught mother whispered, 'Oh no...then please tell me she's fucking ginger and looks the spit of Ed Sheeran. At least that would be something.'

20

'No...she's blonde. She's actually...actually...quite...quite,' she whispered, 'pretty.'

'Noooooooooooo,' the mother let out the mother of all screams before fainting and falling off the bed. The father stood gobsmacked in the corner, butting the concrete wall with the larger of his two heads.

That was the last anyone saw of the couple. Rumour has it, they took their own lives by holding hands and leaping into one of the many pit shafts that littered the mountainside. Others were convinced the village chiefs had intervened to lay down the golden unwritten law of Bedlinog.

'We can't have things like that being born in our community,' grunted one of the village elders at the church meeting the following Sunday, 'we have a reputation to withstand. Imagine what those fuckers from Forchiw would say. We'll be a fuckin' laughing stock.'

After her parent's disappearance, it was left to Dorothy's Aunty Em and Uncle Henry to bring her up. It wasn't easy on the ageing couple.

People would drag their deformed limbs to the other side of the road when they saw Aunty Em' pushing the child down the street in her homemade oil drum pram. The braver ones who dared to glimpse in the pram often screamed out in dismay on seeing the perfectly formed child smiling up at them. When Dorothy reached 4 or 5, Aunty Em would sellotape a brown paper bag over the infant's head when she took her out. On more than one occasion, she'd staple a mask of a deformed monster from the black lagoon to the girl so she wouldn't look out of place when going to school.

On the rare times Aunty Em let her out alone from the basement in their house, deranged kids would stop in the street and yell names at her. Mothers with teeth as sharp as werewolves ushered their own malformed sprogs inside their houses when the pretty girl skipped down the street, humming a tune.

However, after 14 long and painfully abusive years, the residents of Bedlinog finally began to accept the "abnormal" looking girl. Of course, they didn't trust her. Truth be known, they didn't trust anyone. For all the non-Welsh speakers out there reading this, or people who don't know the rich history that flows through the coal seam of this great country, the word Bedlinog translated in Welsh actually means, *the village of ugly freaky in-bred beings who don't trust anyone, never have and never will...full comma, sorry, stop.*

(Told you this book was educational as well as feckin' funny...well, feckin' funny...ish!).

Anyway, that's enough of Dorothy's backstory, let's get back on track, for the second time or this book will turn into a 7 series box set commissioned by Netflix. *(I bloody wish!)*

Still clutching the sheep to its groin, the person in the dirty dungarees, stared at Dorothy and grunted, 'then why won't you marry me then Dorothy? Is it because of my raspy Tom Jones voice?' the individual mimicked the famous singer's voice while jiggling its hips. A mouse tied up in a condom fell out of its trouser leg onto the floor. It tried to wriggle away.

Terry sniffed it and heaved.

'No,' Dorothy lowered the tone of her voice to reply, 'it's not cos of your raspy Tom Jones voice.' She jiggled her hips as well.

'Is it cos of my rough, sheep shearing hands?' Raising its hands in the air, it let go of Doris the sheep. The creature still attached to the person's groin. The look on the sheep's face resembled a man with short arms nailed to a long cross. Well, nailed to a six inch, uncut, with genital warts all over it, cross.

'No,' said Dorothy, 'it's not cos of your rough, sheep shearing hands.'

The person dropped to one knee. The sheep shrieked. 'Then why Dorothy? Why won't you marry me?'

Dorothy sighed, 'Cos Elizabeth, you're my sister.'

Elizabeth got to her feet. She huffed and puffed before storming away. After ten paces, she turned and stormed back. She poked Dorothy

22

in the chest. 'Well, stop pinching all my clothes then, you skinny bitch.' She stormed back off for the second time with the dazed sheep under her arm.

Dorothy shook her beautiful head while skipping off in the opposite direction. 'Come on Terry, let's go and see Aunty Em and Uncle Henry up on the farm. I bet they are doing all farmy type of stuff.'

Dozy Git watched the girl of his dreams disappear off into the distance. Leisurely, he rubbed his chin. 'Dorothy, you will be mine one day...you will be mine.' He grinned as he spied the mouse in the condom struggling about on the ground. Picking it up, he rolled it like a cigar in his sweaty hands before skipping off towards the outhouse, a large erection bursting in his pants.

Chapter 2

CHICKEN FEED

Aunty Em's and Uncle Henry's farm wasn't much to look at. Three acres of baron land balancing on the side of the mountain overlooking the small village. It consisted of an old, rundown shack with walls made from stone dredged up from the river and a roof of rusty corrugated iron sheets bought off the rag and bone man just after the war. It was cold, uncomfortable and damp but it was home to the four of them. Out the back, stood a tiny outhouse surrounded by a picket fence for doing their business. Next to it, a big barn covered in holes where the old couple did some other kind of business, the secret kind; the dirty, secret kind. In the neighbouring fields they owned a few sheep, a goat that looked like Marilyn Manson without his make-up on and a cow with only one leg who hadn't really moved from the same old, oak tree since April 11th 1985.

To call a spade, a shovel, Aunty Em looked much older than her 76 years of age. Wrinkle lines furrowed into her weathered beaten features like tram lines dug into the road on Sheffield High Street. She was short, fat as a space hopper and suffered from a severe case of Tourette's. (Or in her own words, bastard, fucking titty-roll, Tourette's). On the other side of the peculiar family coin, Uncle Henry looked completely the opposite. Tall and skinny, slightly hunched over with enormous ears and one big tooth that protruded out of his mouth like a half-eaten crunchie bar. He only had three fingers on each hand and some stump things that resembled hooves for feet.

The couple had been happily married since they were both 12. In all that time, other than to go to the village for supplies, they had never left the farm. They didn't know that Ystrad Mynach existed, never mind Caerphilly, and Cardiff, may as well be on the moon. Yet like most people of their age, even though they smelt of boiled cabbage and gin, they were happy, and surprisingly healthy in an unhealthy kind of way.

Back up on the farm on that soggy morning, Dorothy skipped merrily through the wooden gate. Terry the dog followed in hot pursuit.

'Aunty Em...Uncle Henry,' she yelled.

She was greeted by silence. She repeated her cry. Still nothing.

From somewhere inside the barn, a loud cackling noise escaped. On tip toes, she inched quietly passed the handwritten sign warning everyone to 'keep out or else'. Unnervingly, she peeked around the door. Almost afraid of what she would see. 'Oh no, I hope they are not having another one of their orgies with that family of travelling circus folk.' Dorothy shivered as she recalled the day she accidently walked in on them in full flow in the long, hot summer of 2006. Individuals of every shape and size, locked together in a saturnalia of flesh, flab and hairy bits. She will never forget the slurping noises. At first, she thought someone had cut the cow's throat. But what she saw, and heard, was much, much worse. Bizarre, sex-crazed characters covered every inch of the floor of the barn. They moaned and groaned and wriggled about like horny worms. In the far corner, a midget dressed as Evil Knievel sat in a small cannon with a dildo strapped to his head. In his hand, a lit match. 'Are you ready Madam...one...two...'

On the other side of the barn, spread-eagled across two bales of hay, greased up like a Christmas turkey, Aunty Em waited in crotch-less beaver skin panties with a big grin on her face.

Dorothy raced out screaming before the cannon fired and the midget flew across the barn, landing dildo first into his intended target.

Even though the disturbing incident took place many years previously, Dorothy still woke up in cold sweats most nights.

Thankfully for her, what she saw in the barn now was a lot more normal, well a lot more normal...ish. There in bright yellow boiler suits with matching gas masks, like a scene from Breaking Bad, stood her guardians. Large, glass test tubes with green liquid circulated around miles of plastic piping lined the length of one of the walls. An oil drum, full to the brim with smelly, toxic, orange liquid smoked and bubbled away in the corner. Balancing on a barrel, an old transistor radio blasted out the song, *'you're the one that I want'* from the movie, *Grease*. Aunty Em and Uncle Henry danced along to the tune.

'Henry, you're the one that I want, you sexy hunk of a man.' Em' purred like a kitten on a stranger's lap.

Uncle Henry shook his butt in the air. 'I'm like a better-looking John Revolter.'

'Aunty Em...Uncle Henry...what are you doing?' Dorothy broke the mood.

The couple stopped.

In one movement, they turned to face her.

'Nothing, Dorothy,' removing her mask, Aunty Em grunted. Her eyes bloodshot. Sweat dripped off her little, grey moustache. 'We're busy Dorothy...now go away. FUCKFACED CRAB!'

Dorothy shrugged and began to leave the barn.

For a canine, Terry was quite clued up on the workings of the underworld. He sensed something wasn't quite right. He barked.

Dorothy picked him up to her ear. 'What did you say, Terry? You think we are in a...' the dog yapped louder, 'a lab...a maths lab...you say!'

(Right, right, right... before you write a letter to my publisher to complain about how the hell a girl could understand a dog. She couldn't understand dog. It was a trick she had learned. Being quite shy, she often used the dog's barking as a way of asking the awkward questions

27

which she couldn't bring herself to ask. This often-got poor Terry in trouble).

Uncle Henry growled at the innocent creature. Aunty Em flicked out her lizard shaped tongue full of venom and hate.

'Sorry Terry, what did you say,' Dorothy continued, 'not a maths lab...a meths lab.' She folded her arms. 'Uncle Henry, Aunty Em...you ain't cooking up crystal meths again, are you?'

'A chance would be a fine thing,' Aunty Em replied, 'POOPHEADS...of course, we ain't cooking up Crystal fuckin' Meths, ARSEBANDITS. This is Bedlinog, not fuckin' Newport city centre...TITTY TITTY BANG COCKS.'

'Well, what's all this then?'

Uncle Henry piped up. 'Scchhhhh...come here...we're making.' He looked about suspiciously before lowering his tone, 'special chicken feeeeeeeeeed.'

'Special...what?'

'Special chicken feeeeeeeeeeeed,' Aunty Em joined Henry in the 'feeeeeeeed' part.

'What's so special about it?' Even though it was still quite early in the day, Dorothy could smell the turps on her Uncle's breath.

'Remember little Edwina Curry,' Aunty Em intervened, 'your pet hen?' Dorothy closed her eyes. She instantly pictured her favourite, miniscule, adorable pet hen waddling around their farm during the sunniest day of the summer. She nodded, 'well look at her now.' Em' shone a torch high up into the darkness of the chicken coup above their heads.

Dorothy shrieked.

There, alone in the darkness, sat an enormous ten-foot chicken with feet as big as clown's shoes. The light from the torch caused the deformed creature to let go of a high-pitched startled screech. It pooped out a gargantuan egg.

'Yes, that's my girl,' yelled Aunty Em, 'the scramble eggs are on Edwina.'

'My, oh my.' Dorothy backed away, 'isn't that dangerous?'

Uncle Henry burped. 'Only if you get it drunk on Strongbow. Anyway,' he pointed at the dog. 'He's the only dangerous thing around here.'

'Terry?'

'Yeah.'

'Why?'

'Tell her, Em.'

The old woman shook her head violently. 'Dorothy, love, Miss Slocombe called around today...and she's not too pleased. FUCK...FUCKBUTTCHEEKS.'

'Miss Slocombe...Why?

'Cos that mutt's been messing about with Miss Slocombe's,' Uncle Henry spat out his words like a fly had flown into his mouth, 'uhm...her pussy...that's why.'

Other than old Dai Half-a-Spade, the farmer who grew fields full of cannabis which he turned into space cakes at Easter, Miss Slocombe was the most powerful individual in the entire village. She may have been the village drunk, who surrounded herself with hordes of manky cats, but she was also the only qualified pig-whisperer for a radius of over 15 miles. So even though she smelt of undiluted cat piss, she was held in high esteem amongst the community. Everyone did their best not to upset her. Upset Miss Slocombe and a pig would die!!

'Miss Slocombe's pussy,' Dorothy mumbled again.

'YES!'

Terry, the cat hater (or maybe, Terry, the cat lover) tried to silently tip toe towards the barn door.

Looking quite confused, Dorothy faced her relatives. 'But I don't understand...what would Terry do with Miss Slocombe's pussy?'

'You know!'

'I don't, Uncle Henry...don't forget I'm only 14.'

'Only 14,' Aunty Em shrieked like an insane banshee. 'I'd given birth to 8 kids, 2 goats, TWATS...and worked part-time in Aldi.'

'Beep...beep...beep,' Uncle Henry insanely mimicked a girl sitting at the check-out till. He scanned invisible items through the invisible barcoding machine. 'Cleaning assistant required in aisle...aisle...aisle...sevennnnnnnnnnnnnn,' he howled.

'FUCKING FUCK FUCKERS,' Aunt Em yelled, 'and that was before they had barcoding, when I was 14, my girl,' she added, 'now stop being so naïve, that dirty mutt has been giving Miss Slocombe's pussy a length of his...his old red bloody lipstick...BASTARD CHOPS.'

All eyes stared at the dog. Dorothy picked it up. 'His what?'

'His red lipstick...you know,' Dorothy shook her head. Aunty Em squealed louder. 'His old todger, his magic wand, his poking stick, his Mutton dagger, FUCK...his Spam javelin, his Taco warmer, his Gash mallet.' Has she spoke, in the background, Uncle Henry did all of the actions. 'His Whore thermometer, his Vlad the Impaler, his Puff the one-eyed dragon, his Womb ferret, COCK ROT...his Slit-eyed demon...FANNY LIPS.' Out of breath, she panted. 'That!' she pointed at the dog's dick.

'Oh...his wax remover.'

Uncle Henry cried out in rage. 'His what?'

'Terry uses that thing to remove wax from my ears...he said it's the best way.... look' She gently inserted the dog's penis into her ear and twigged it around.

The dog closed it eyes. It let go of a soft moan.

Aunty Em slapped the beast around the head. 'I bet he does...well he better keep his dirty old "wax remover" in his little old doggy speedos from now on...Miss Slocombe's pussy had kittens this morning...Look at these.' She handed Dorothy a photograph of a cat surrounded by a posse of tiny kittens. All the new kittens had faces identical to Terrys.

'Terry...couldn't have done that.'

'He did...TWAT PUSS...and it's not the first time either. Last month, WANKER...there was Old Charlie the farmer.' She handed over another Polaroid. This time it showed a gang of new born lambs who again all looked suspiciously like the horny old mutt.

'And don't forget, young Chantelle's baby boy,' piped up Uncle Henry. 'Poor Chantelle.'

The black and white photo showed a young, toothless teenage girl sitting up in bed clutching a baby with a rather doggy looking face.

'But Terry's just friendly...that's all,' Dorothy chuckled.

'That's one way of putting it...BASTARD PAWS. Now, Dorothy it's the school holidays so you need to find a place where you and that mutt don't get into trouble...otherwise it will be SNIP!' she made a gesture like a pair of scissor snapping closed, 'off with his "Wax remover" MINGE HEAD, CLITTY CLIT.'

Terry glanced down at his own penis. All the sex talk had made him rather horny. He prayed his old lipstick wouldn't been sticking out. But he knew it would be. And it was. It stuck out like a rampant windsock in a hurricane. He covered it up with his paw. His cheeks as red as his throbbing lipstick.

'Don't say that Aunty Em...you'll scare him.'

'SCARE HIM...SCARE HIM...castrate the dirty, hairy, horny, little fucker I should...the little...CU...CUN...CUN...C you next Tuesday!' Before marching out of the barn, she booted a big, fluffy, four foot rabbit out of her way. Uncle Henry hobbled behind her.

Dorothy looked at the dog. 'Come here boy...I don't believe a word they said about you...you are a good boy, you wouldn't go near any of these animals, especially Chantelle Lewis. She's a right bike, I heard.'

Terry looked away all sheepish. He leapt up into her arms. The girl walked out of the barn into the daylight.

'Some place where we won't get into trouble, Terry.' She placed the creature on the old damaged wagon wheel leaning up against the barn wall. 'Do you suppose there is such a place? There must be. I bet it's not a place you can get to by boat or by train. It's far, far away, behind the moon...beyond the rain, turn sharp left at Pontypridd railway station. That's where my dream place is Terry. Did you know, when all the clouds darken up the skyway, there's a rainbow highway to be found. Leading from your window pane. Just a step beyond the rain...look.'

'What the fish fingers is she on about now?' Terry thought to itself, 'she must have been on the glue again.'

Dorothy pulled a tattered tourist board brochure out of her school bag. With her eyes alive with hope, she flicked through the pages. 'See Terry...this is the place we should go.' She scanned the photos of exotic sounding places like Penhrys, Ystrad and Tonypandy. She beamed at the images on every page of the coloured magazine of fat girls in G-strings and blokes holding pints of weak beer while posing in brown and white chequered suits like detectives from the 70's. 'Let me tell you about it...better still let me sing you a song about it, Terry.'

The dog rolled his eyes. 'Oh no, not another bloody song.'

But it was too late, Dorothy's voice pierced the afternoon sky. 'Somewhere over the Rhondda, steroid sales are high, there's a crazy land that I heard of...where roidheads are all called Dai.'

Unknown to her, all the animals came out of their hiding places to listen to the girl with the voice of an angel. Her lyrics transporting them all too some magical land far, far away.

A vulture landed on the nearby fence.

Dorothy continued singing away. 'Somewhere over the Rhondda, where the mothers ain't shy, they all go Valley Commando, don't stare or you'll get black eye.' Terry got another erection. 'One day I'll get drunk in a bar and wake up where the fashion is 10 years behind me, girls in pencil skirts and tight boob-tops, buy heroin from front room shops, that's where you'll find me. Somewhere over the Rhondda, steroid sales are high, there's a crazy land that I heard of...where roidheads are all called Dai.'

A mouse wiped a small tear away from its eye and stood up on an old wheelbarrow to clap. The vulture swooped over and gobbled it up in one go. The bird burped as it sailed high up into the sky. Dorothy watched it disappear over the slag heap towards Trelewis.

'That's where we should go Terry...the Rhondda...I heard they have thousands of exotic shops there called Poundshops that stretch as far as the eye can see. And what's more everything they sell in there is a...pound.'

The dog tutted and muttered to itself. 'Yeah, that's why they are called Poundshops, you moron.'

Aunty Em appeared from the kitchen holding a freshly killed badger in one hand and a cut-throat razor in the other. Blood dripped down her arm and onto her pink croc shoes. 'Dorothy, stop all that day dreaming my girl, you won't have time for travelling when you marry Dozy Git.'

'No! Aunty Em...I don't want to marry Dozy Git...I want to marry some prince.'

'We all wanted to marry Prince.' The elderly lady drifted off into some sort of sexual trance, rubbing her private parts with the head of the dead animal. She wailed, *'you don't have to be beautiful to turn me on...I just need your body, baby, from dusk till dawn.'* She snapped back to normality. 'Fuck me...that man was like a three-foot vibrator. NIPPLE RINGS. So, my girl, you are marrying Dozy Git and that's the last I want to hear about it...now get upstairs and help shave your sister's back.' She held out a rusty razor.

Dorothy looked at the shaving device, and then at the dead badger. She picked up the dog. 'I will never marry Dozy Git. Quick Terry, let's get outta here.' She raced off as fast as her legs could carry her. She sprinted passed the gargoyle weathervane towards the dark wood with the skinny, Eastern European trees. She knew exactly where she was heading, but she wasn't sure how to get there.

Aunty Em watched her go. 'We should have drowned the twat at birth...MONKEY-RIMMED PENIS,' she muttered and walked towards the old farm house.

Chapter 3
MAD DOGS AND PERVY MEN

Out of breath, Dorothy stumbled onwards through the darkening forest. She ran passed a burnt out 1978 Ford Fiesta. Then they passed the tree that looked like an arse. She picked up Terry and ankle-high, she paddled through the lime green coloured river polluted by the waste from the nearby biscuit factory. Overhead, the sky got darker as the storm clouds came out to play.

'I hope we don't see any creatures, or pervy men, or morons, sorry, Mormons, Terry,' she whispered to her best friend. The dog looked right and left. He knew he had to keep his wits about him. He'd heard the rumours of what the men of a place called Blackwood did with stray animals. It was enough to make one's eyes water, and not in a good way!

Just at that moment, the skies reverberated with an enormous crack as a loud burp of thunder shook the Valley to its core. Seconds later, a bolt of lightning made her jump. The rain lashed down. The wind blew a gale. A small hurricane crept its way up the Valley, destroying everything in its path. She cwtched the frightened dog up in her arms. Several items of cheap, plastic garden furniture sailed passed them.

'Oh no Terry...it's a twister...it's a twister.' Debris of all shapes and sizes littered the sky. Traffic cones, trees, fencing, a motorbike, wheelie bins and a small boy in a canoe sailed past her. She ducked down just in time as an 18 stone pig clenching for dear life to a fence post came into view before disappearing into the darkness. Panting for breath and scared out of her wits, her and Terry took shelter behind a huge conker tree. Seconds later, a lightning bolt shook the old sapling to its roots. It slowly toppled over, crashing to the ground. Dorothy screamed and ran and ran and ran. The eye of the storm got closer and closer. Large droplets of rain obscured her view. It made her journey even slower and a lot more dangerous.

About twenty minutes later, they took shelter in a beaten-up bus stop which as usual smelt of piss and desperation. Soaking wet she cuddled up to Terry to try and stop the poor creature from catching its death.

Out of nowhere, she heard a noise.

She froze.

It sounded like someone dragging their feet across a shag pile carpet. From the shadows, four teenagers appeared. Dorothy gasped on seeing their unfortunate appearance. They seemed to be cover from head to toe in thick, matted, black hair. In sheer terror Dorothy pushed back up against the wall of the shelter. Too afraid to scream out, she covered her face. She had heard about the hairy people of Treharris but always thought it was an urban myth told to her by her Aunty to stop her venturing out of the village.

The biggest and most hairy of the gang members approached her. His stare fixed on the girl and her dog. Dorothy held her breath. Terry covered his eyes. When the boy got a few feet away, he muttered, 'you haven't got a Mach 3 razor I can borrow have you, love?' the poor boy asked, his eyes filled his tears. Dorothy shook her head. 'How about a Gillette Fusion Proglide, then?'

'No, sorry.'

Another one stepped out into the grey light and hissed, 'Even a fuckin' Bic razor will do, love. We know it will cut us to ribbons, but anything will be better than living like this. I don't want to be hairy anymore...please.' He grabbed out at Dorothy's arm.

Terry snapped at the hairy teenager.

The kids backed away.

'Or even a small tube of Immac?' asked another. Dorothy suspected this one was either a girl or an actual gorilla in a tight Primark boob-top and stretched jeans.

'No, I haven't sorry...honest. Have you tried Boots?'

'Boots...Boots...this is Treharris, Love...not fucking New York City. We haven't even got a corner shop cos of him,' the first hairy boy pointed at one of the kids at the back in Bill Stunt stretch jeans.

'Don't blame me,' the boy replied.

'But you burnt the shop down.'

'Well he refused to serve me ten Woodbine and a party can of Double Diamond'

'Cos you ain't old enough to buy fags.'

'But I had an ID.'

'Oh, fuck off Derek...it was a fake ID, you know it was and he knew it as well.'

'It wasn't fake, Neil.'

'Derek it was. You used a Blockbuster video card and just stuck a photo of Galen from Planet of the Apes on it.'

'I didn't. It was me.'

'It was Galen.'

The hairy kids started to bicker amongst themselves. Dorothy took the opportunity to leg it. Racing passed the Navigation Arms pub, she headed off down the high street, turning left up a side street and into a series of fields. Lost and afraid, girl and dog walked aimlessly through the long grass. The cold wind wrapped itself around her skinny bones and refused to let go.

'I'm scared Terry...shall we go back.' She slumped down on a tree stump, tears rolled down her cheeks.

'Hey love, what's wrong?' a man with dyed blond shoulder length hair in a shiny, purple and white track suit stood next to a caravan. On the side of the blue vehicle the words, *'Professor Jimmy – been fixing it for children the world over since 1971'* arrogantly stood out in yellow letters. The man puffed on a huge cigar. Smoked bellowed up in the air.

'Hey Mister Jimmy...I'm Dorothy and this is Terry and we are lost and I'm scared.'

The man fiddled with the large gold chain around his neck. 'Come inside my girl, take the weight off your feet...Professor Jimmy is here to help.' He motioned for her to follow him into the van. Terry barked, and pulled at her white ankle sock. Dorothy was too tired to listen. She needed shelter and some food. She followed the man into his flat in Leeds, where he proceeded to drug her then rape her, no sorry, she followed the man into his caravan somewhere in South Wales.

'Come and sit down, love,' Professor Jimmy said. Dorothy went to sit in the seat opposite him. 'No, me dear...sit here,' he rubbed his thighs, 'come on, I won't bite...well unless you want me too.'

'What?'

'Nothing, love...only messing about. That's a nice pussy you got.'

'What?'

Terry the dog growled at him.

'No, that's not a pussy cat...that's Terry...Terry the dog.'

'I wasn't talking about,' he stopped, 'oh yeah...the dog...he's cute.' He smirked. 'Better get my eyes tested. Now come sit and tell Professor Jimmy all about it.' The caravan filled with cigar smoke.

Reluctantly the girl sat down on the old pervy's legs. Due to the shiny material of his trousers, she slipped off onto the floor.

'Ooooooooooo, you little tease,' the man let go of a moaning sound. 'How old are you my love, 16 or 17?'

'No...I'm only 14?' She sat back down on his lap.

'OOOOOOOO...OOOOOOO...OOOOOOOO.' a big grin widened his face. He looked up to the heavens. 'Ooooooooo...Ooooooooooo...thank you the god known as Ted Heath...thank you so much.'

The girl shuffled about awkwardly on his lap. 'Sorry Mister Jimmy...I think I've just sat on your weird shaped cigar in your pocket.'

The creepy man held up his Cuban. 'I don't think you have me love?' he sniggered and blew a ring of smoke into her face. 'Maybe I'm just pleased to see you.'

'AAAARRRGGGGHHHHHH,' she screamed and leapt to her feet. She was quite naive but even she could sense something wasn't right.

The man reached out to grab her. Terry jumped up on the table and bite down hard on Professor Jimmy's finger.

'Ooooooooo now then, now then,' the man yelped, 'there's no need to get rough.'

The young girl barged open the caravan door. She and her dog raced off into a bright yellow corn field which had sprung up overnight just outside Edwardsville. She rushed through the vegetation, afraid to look back.

From behind her, she could hear the yells of the old, pervy man. 'Now then, now then...come back little girl...Jim with fix it for you...I promise.'

She ran as fast as she could. Not sure where she was going but she didn't care. She just needed to get away. Terry the dog raced in front of her. He stopped abruptly on seeing a cute looking squirrel fiddling with its nuts. Looking straight ahead, Dorothy tripped over the horny mutt and rolled down a hill. Landing at the feet of a man with a small goatee beard, holding a paint brush, she looked up.

He opened up his dirty, old rain coat to expose himself. He hissed, 'Do you know what it is yet?' in a strange put-on Australian accent.

'Arrgghhhhhhhhh,' she screamed again.

She raced down the steep banking until she came to a deserted road. Off in the distance, the smoke from a series of big industrial chimneys filled the air with smog.

'Look Terry...it's our dream...quick...hurry...It's the Rhondda.'

Chapter 4

I DON'T THINK WE'RE IN BEDLINOG ANYMORE, TERRY!

The town clock that loomed down on the busy town centre informed Dorothy it was 6.45 in the morning as her and Terry wandered into Merthyr High Street. Actually, the right time was five past 2 in the afternoon. The town clock hadn't worked for yonks. Not since the council sacked the dozen or so council workers responsible for maintaining the clocks during the second great council budget cuts of '98. In that savage second wave of redundancies they also binned all the lollypop women. Most of them were touching 78, so it was probably safer for the kid's anyway. Also, they got rid of the army of grass cutters, a bus load of the bell ringers, the head of the councillor's food tasters, the toilet seat warmers, several of the YTS scheme teenagers who fed the fish in reception, and the odd couple who made bees honey on the roof of the council building which the councillors spread on their toast every morning. (They didn't get rid of the toast makers, or the honey spreaders though).

Dorothy walked on the unkempt grass under the railway bridge. She glanced up at the big, white cloth dangling off the iron structure. The bed sheet which some proud kid (or kids) had handmade, wished their grandmother, Theresa, a very happy 32nd Birthday. In smaller letters underneath, they also hoped her new 36 double D boob job had been a massive success.

That afternoon, the small narrow street proved to be a hive of activity. Market traders, standing on tiptoes on wooden boxes, screamed out at shoppers to come and sample their wares. Hundreds of stalls snaked their way up the street like a giant, tarpaulin covered python.

Everything under the sun could be brought. Fake clothes, fake passports, fake tan, stolen meat, illegal drugs, legal drugs, cigars, fags, e-cigs, fruit machines, white socks of various shades of white, stretchy boob tops (one size only) and racks and racks of birthday cards for every occasion.

'Roll up...roll up,' one trader bellowed, 'I have more real, fake items than any bloody flea infested market in Marmaris in Turkey.' The small crowd around his stall clapped and cheered before pulling their money out to buy anything that looked good, bad or ugly.

Outside Nat West bank, two Big Issue Seller jostled each other for the best spot. The scabby dog of the bigger Big Issue Seller bit the scabbier dog of the smaller Big Issue Seller. A fight broke out between men and beasts.

Dorothy walked on into a swarm of shoppers ambling about. Most of them riding on mobility scooters, fags in mouths and with carrier bags full of cheap cat food on the handlebars. One extremely large lady in a souped-up scooter run over Dorothy's foot. 'Ouch!' the girl yelped.

'Well, get out of me way, you thick twat,' the shopper yelled, 'there's a sale on at Poundland.'

'That's not very nice,' Dorothy replied.

'Eat my shit,' the woman sped off, skidding around the corner on two wheels.

The young girl winced in pain and hobbled off through the crowd. She stopped at the back of a long queue of unemployed teenage couples standing outside a glamorous looking building.

'What's going on in there?' she asked a girl in pyjama bottoms, smoking a fag and rocking a pram with a new born baby in it.

'It's the Pandora shop, love...it's magical. This one is buying me,' she motioned to her boyfriend next to her standing in a gold and white track suit and baseball hat, 'a big fuck off diamond ring, that's what he's buying me.' The boy growled at her. 'Don't look at me like that...it's your fucking fault, you shouldn't have shagged my best mate...should you have?' she turned to Dorothy. 'Top tip babes, get your boyfriend to shag your mate and you can get a ring as well...look at these.' She flashed her both hands which were covered in cheap silver and gold rings. 'Oh!' she yelled at a girl in front of her, 'Oh you, fat fuck, stop cheating the queue.'

'I ain't.'

'You is...isn't she?' she asked Dorothy. Dorothy shrugged. 'You are cheating so get back or I'll fucking smash you.'

There ensued a full-on, stare out between the girls for a full minute and a half, before the girl who cheated the queue, marched at the back, pushing her pram. 'Least my boyfriend hasn't been fucking about again.'

'Yeah...only cos your boyfriend likes sucking cock.'

'He doesn't.'

'He does...doesn't he?' she motioned to Dorothy again. Dorothy shrugged again.

'Is it now,' the cheating girl yelled.

The both girls raced at each other, prams first. They smashed into each other. The new born babies started screaming. The girls started fighting.

Dorothy hurried away. 'There must be very rich people living here Terry...did you see the jewellery on those girls...very rich indeed.'

'Never mind rich...there seems to be loads of shagging going on here,' Terry grinned to himself.

Outside a café, sitting on aluminium chairs, a gang of old ladies gathered, smoking like chimneys, drinking tea like China-men while moaning about the weather, their husbands and the price of corned beef.

'Out of the fuckin' way,' a shoplifter in brand new Nike trainers, clutching a stolen 48-inch TV under his arms, pushed passed Dorothy. A store detective in shiny black slip-ons followed in hot pursuit. The detective reached out to grab the thief but slipped and crashed into a man selling accident insurance.

'The fuckin' irony,' the shoplifter laughed and stuck his two fingers up before disappearing up the alley towards the train station.

The store detective got to his feet. 'I hate this job,' he said to Dorothy, 'look at the shoes they gave me...just look at 'em,' he cried, 'I couldn't catch a pig in a fucking passage with these on.' Head lowered in defeat yet again, he stomped back to the shop to write a letter of complaint about his inappropriate, company issue footwear.

'Oh, look Terry,' Dorothy said, 'there's one of those Poundshops over there,' She walked on. 'And that other shop is a betting office. That one is a charity shop and that other one is a mobile phone shop.' They walked on ten yards. 'Oh, look Terry, another Poundshop...but this one is called Poundworld, and there's another betting office. And another charity shop....and a shop selling phones.' They walked on. 'Oh, look Terry...this one is called Cheaper Poundland....and there's another....' Suddenly she stopped dead in her tracks.

'YOU!' An old street preacher in a 1940's hat, his body encased in a board proclaiming 'the world would end a week on Wednesday after the One Show', pointed at the girl.

Dorothy refused to catch his glare.

'You, I'm talking to,' he shrieked, 'are going to Hell, bitch,' he yelled at her, 'Hell...I'm telling you.' He unscrewed a small brown bottle and threw water over Terry. 'Pray to the lord...pray to the lord. You and your devil goat, pray to the lord.' He spat as he talked.

'Excuse me sir...Terry's not a goat, he's a dog.'

'It looks like a goat and it smells like a goat, so it is a goat...and you smell like a...' he took a deep breath, 'you smell like a tuna sandwich...you're both going to Heeeeeeeelllllllllllllllllllllllllllllll.' He added so many L's that by the time he finished she was covered in phlegm.

Scared shitless and wiping spit from her eyes, the frightened girl legged it down an alleyway. Finding a gap in a wooden board in an abandoned old furniture shop, she crawled in. Tired and hungry she rolled up into a ball and cried herself to sleep. Terry laid near her feet.

Hours later, she woke with a jump. She looked about for her shoes. They had gone.

'Terry...Terry,' the dog lay fast sleep, his lipstick fully sticking out of its hairy container. 'Fine bloody guard dog you are...someone's stolen my shoes.'

'Uhmmmm...what?' the dog looked startled. It looked about. 'For fuck sake,' he barked to itself. 'I was just about to nail Pamela Anderson and her twin brother...and you woke me up cos someone stole your fucking shoes. ARRGGHHHHHH. They were made from the bark of a fucking tree...aaarrggghhhhh.' He put his head in his paws. 'Come back Pamela...I will be your Tommy Lee...or Terry Lee...woof.'

Barefoot, she ventured outside the building. Terry followed, still barking small barks to himself. It was dark outside, but no less noisy. A different and more violent throng of populace had replaced the happy shoppers on their mobility scooters and teenagers covered in love-bites and false diamonds.

Loud music blasted out from nearby pubs packed with drunks looking for action, of any kind. Bouncers stood in doorways, telling punters to, fuck off and come back when they were out of short trousers. A few scuffles broke out in the street. A police car drove by ignoring the commotion. A line of taxis kerb-crawled the streets looking for customers.

Dorothy and Terry moved from doorway to doorway, trying not to be seen. A gang of rowdy girls dressed up in pink tee-shirts with slogans

45

on the back such as 'Helen the cock monster', or 'Debra does Dowlais Rugby Club' staggered passed them. One girl covered in dunkies carried a blow-up doll of a man with a huge moustache and a huger erect penis. Nosily, the girls headed to Wetherspoons. One of the females grabbed a bouncer by the balls and yelled out, 'Fuck my dead gran...you don't get many of those to the pound.'

All her friends cackled like witches and marched into the pub.

Afraid to move, Dorothy hid in a doorway of Chickenland. She didn't notice that someone with a dry sense of humour and access to spray paint had painted over the chicken part of the sign with the words Munkin. A large poster in the window announced, "tonites special offer, 10 chicken wings for the price of 11".

'I'm hungry, Terry,' Dorothy sniffed the air, 'but we ain't got any money.'

Two teenage boys sauntered towards her. The bigger and fatter one dressed in a gold coloured shell suit with a Burberry baseball cap, worn the wrong way around, spoke in a loud and threatening manner to his mate. 'I told you not to shit on your own doorstep, Butt...didn't I?'

Shoulders hunched over, his sidekick, in similar gear but in silver, replied, 'Yeah, but I didn't think she would catch me pochin' with her sister, did I?'

The thug boy stopped and yelled out. 'Potching with her sister. Butt, they've got fuckin' bunk beds mun. She'll have you down Pandora tomorrow morning, first thing, buying her a 'sorry I shagged your sister' gift. That's gonna cost you big style. I reckon, a bracelet, two diamante nipple rings, and a pearl necklace at least...anyway I'm starving...you hungry?

'Yeah, but I better go see the Mrs mun.'

'Fuck her mate...she's probably up Big Ken's rubbing his body in chip fat as we speak. Look, how's about me and you going £3.20 each and we'll go down Ally Ally McAlly's kebab shop for a super-duper mega wrap is it?'

46

'Oi...go on then.'

They started to walk passed the doorway. Thug boy stopped, 'I need a slash first.'

He pulled down the front of his trackee. His dark yellow, warm pee gushed down between the cracks in the broken pavement. Not to be left out, his sidekick followed suit. *(No, he didn't gush down the cracks in the broken pavement like dark yellow, warm piss. He also had a wazz).* Thug boy stared at Dorothy. 'Who the fuck is you looking at, Butt?'

His sidekick chipped in, 'Looking at, Butt?'

The girl shook her head. 'No one.'

'Looks like you is. Well take a photo then love, it will last longer.'

'Last longer,' Sidekick copied.

With their cocks still exposed to the elements, the two boys glared at the girl.

'My red lipstick is bigger than the both of those,' Terry smirked to himself, 'put together. I could poke that skinny one's girlfriend and her sister.' Terry moaned out in pleasure.

Dorothy picked the dog up. 'Quick Terry...I've got a feeling we're not in Bedlinog anymore.' She sprinted up the high street. Two men in their late fifties, stripped to the waist, squared up to each in the middle of the road.

'I'll fucking beat you to within an inch of your life,' the stockier man shouted in an Irish accent. 'No one eats my chicken tenders.'

'You ate my fuckin' chips,' came back the reply.

'They were fuckin' stone cold.'

'You will be stone fuckin' cold now in a fuckin' minute.'

A punch connected.

A Copper parked up eating a burger in a lay-by beeped his horn in time to the punches being thrown. The rest of the people on the High Street ignored the fighting men and went about their business. Dorothy swiftly headed away from the aggro. Her taste buds took her towards the weird looking Chinese restaurant that shone like a beacon among a gang of kebab houses and next door to an old woman's clothes boutique which had a 'closing down, everything must go' sign in the window for the past twenty-two years.

It wasn't until the smell of the delights of the food tickled her nostrils did she realise just how hungry she was. Terry felt the same.

Dorothy peeked through the dirty net curtain draped on the eatery door. The room looked full to the brim. Most of the tables were occupied. Some bald bloke lay flat out on the floor, face down. A woman in white stilettoes and slutty looking white clothes staggered from out of the toilets. The back of her dress caught in her underwear. Her pink G-string winked at punters as she stepped over the bloke on the ground.

'They let some fucking riff raff in here,' she grunted while flicking her V's up at the couple on the far table trying to hide behind the grimy looking menus.

'Don't look at her, Ernie...don't look at her,' the Mayor's wife hissed under her breath.

The Mayor pretended to scan the menu.

'I won't turn you into fucking stone...you ugly twats.' The slutty woman in white shoes stumbled towards the table in the opposite corner. She snarled at everyone before sitting down. 'I want grub,' she yelled out, 'give me my grub.' She banged on the table.

The door to the kitchen shot open. Glinda strolled out like John Wayne promenading up Boot Hill to have a gun fight with a gang of baddies with shifty eyes and black hats. In one hand, she held a plate of fried rice, whilst with the other she scratched her arse as if she was finger digging for gold.

Ever since the Chinese had opened twenty-odd years earlier, Glinda had been, and still was, the only non-Chinese person to work in the infamous restaurant. Probably about 45 years old, she looked at least 15 years older. The grey roots poking through her dyed blonde hair was matched only by the colour of her dirty, yellow nicotine stained fingers. A mother of six, she survived up on the Galon Uchaf estate by earning a little cash as the estate's agony aunt and part-time psychic.

The room fell quiet.

Glinda prowled amongst the eaters. No one dared to catch her glare. By the time she got to the slut in white, the obnoxious, drunken woman had collapsed asleep. Her head flat down on the red and white checked tablecloth. Glinda didn't bat an eyelash. She lifted the woman's head up by her hair and threw the plate of special fried rice, with a large fried egg on top of it, on the table.

'One...two...three,' she let the woman's head go. SPLATT. Her face landed in the nosh. She didn't even stir, never mind, wake up.

Glinda waddled away, sniffing her fingers.

'Excuse me Miss...Miss,' the Mayor held up his hand.

'What?' Glinda grunted.

The Mayor pointed at the second page of the menu. 'Can you tell me please, what is the difference between a Hing Hong special and a special Hing Hongs?'

Glinda's sigh could be heard above the noise and peculiar Chinese background music. 'Yeah...a Hing Hongs special comes with only two fried eggs on top of it, love.'

The Mayor's wife, in her Sunday best and newly done bee-hive hair-do, piped up, 'A fried what?

'A fried fucking egg, love,' Glinda didn't mince her words, 'you get them out of chicken's arses.' She squatted down in front of their table and pretended to lay an egg. She farted loudly, not once but twice. She fanned her hand in front of her face. 'Now that's what you call a double yolker!'

Outside the door, Dorothy's stomach rumbled. 'Shall we go in, Terry?' The dog licked its hungry lips.

Gently, she opened the door and entered. The bell on the entrance let go of a haunting sound. Everyone turned and stared at the young girl with no shoes on her feet, holding a little dog.

Ten seconds of silence followed.

'You can't bring a fucking rat in here,' Glinda muttered.

'Yeah...all the rats are to go in the kitchen. Killed, skinned and put in the chicken stroke, rat curry, half and half.' The amusing youngster in the Wrangler jacket's laugh was short lived. A spoon gripped firmly by the waitress smashed across the joker's head.

'Ouch!'

'Shut your fucking mouth...this place has been shut down six times this month already.'

Dorothy whispered. 'But it's not a rat...it's a dog, Terry the dog.'

'Oh, that's fine then.' Glinda grabbed Dorothy's arm. 'Are you hungry, love?' Dorothy nodded. Glinda murmured. 'Well if I was you...I'd go to the kebab shop across the street...these kitchens are fuckin' stinking. There's a cockroach in the women's toilets bigger than your fucking rat, sorry, your dog....and the chef's got the shits.'

A drunk man spat his food back up onto the table. Glinda growled at him. No one moved. Using his spoon, the man scooped the mess up.

'Eat it!' Glinda stated.

The man did what he was told. He chewed while faking a smile.

'But...but...but I haven't got any money,' Dorothy stood there, almost in tears.

'Oh, why didn't you say that?' Glinda showed the girl to an empty table by the bar. She bounded over to the woman in white. She picked up her head, wiped some rice and egg yolk off her face back onto the plate. She walked back to the girl and handed her the plate. She spat on the spoon, cleaned it in her apron and said. 'Get that down you...by the way, I'm Glinda.'

'Thank you, Glinda...I'm Dorothy.' She started eating the food. She handed a mouth full to Terry. He looked at it and shook his head. Dorothy glanced around the room. 'Is this the Rhondda?'

There was a loud gasp. Then everyone in the room, except one, shouted out in unison. 'FUCK OFF...The Rhondda...do we look like a bunch of steroid heads?'

A steroidhead, sitting near the door, whipped his top off. He flexed his oversized muscles. 'Oh, what's wrong with Steriodheads from the Rhondda?'

'Hang on everyone,' Glinda rolled her eyes. She marched over to the roidhead. 'Oi Dai...get out.'

'How do you know my name was Dai?' he replied.

'Haven't you read the poster?' she pointed to the massive poster on the wall. It stated in large letters in English, Welsh and Polish, *the following things are not allowed inside this establishment: Guns, cameras, mobiles, rats, councillors, or Steroidheads from the Rhondda (called Dai).* 'Of course, you haven't...you probably can't fucking read. Now FUCK OFF.'

The roidhead stood his ground. The veins in his forehead ready to pop.

Glinda pulled back her apron to reveal a small, black handgun. 'You want some, big boy.'

The roidhead didn't budge.

'I bet you're wondering if this is a real gun or a novelty salt cellar...ain't you punk. Are you man enough to find out?'

The tension was unbearable. No one moved. Glinda's hand twitched by her weapon. In one movement, the roidhead kicked over the table and rushed out as fast as he could. His tail firmly between his legs. Glinda turned to Dorothy. 'No love...this isn't the Rhondda. This is Merffa...the best and most cultured place in all the whole of the Valleys.'

'Hello Miss,' the Mayor's wife interrupted her, 'can we have a pot of Chinese tea for two, please?'

Some of the customers giggled. Some stared. Some ducked down under the table. Glinda stamped down hard on a cockroach. She pushed her tits together. 'Hang on a sec, love,' she apologised to Dorothy. Pretending to be a primate scratching under her armpits, she swayed over to the table. She faced the posh couple. 'Do I look like the fucking monkey off the Tyhoo tea advert? Well, do I? Well, I'm not...so we haven't got any

Chinese tea, or Yorkshire Tea, or Typhoo tea. This is Hing Hongs not a fucking cafe...Now get out...you're both banned.' The couple refused to move. 'OUT, I SAID!'

The Mayor stood up, smashing his hand down in anger onto the table. He strutted like a peacock in bloom to the centre of the room. 'You can't ban me...I'm the Mayor,' he announced, whilst attempting some royal pose he had practised many times in his bedroom mirror. He lifted his right arm up into the air, his other hand on his hip.

The Mayor's wife scuttled after him. She gripped his arm. 'And I'm the Mayor's wife.' She did the same pose as her husband of over forty years.

Without a moment's hesitation, Glinda pulled the handgun out from under her apron. Uncocking the safety catch, she barged between them. 'I don't care if you're David Beckham.' She pointed the gun at the Mayor, 'and she's skinny fucking, thinny fucking, Minnie Spice...now get out, you're banned.' The couple looked at each other. They grabbed their stuff and headed for the door. Glinda added, 'banned I said...well, except for Mondays...it is quiet on Mondays.' Panting like a wild boar, Glinda turned back to Dorothy, gun still in her hand, 'Where are you from, love?'

'Bedlinog.'

Glinda whistled the opening bars of duelling banjos. 'Well, I hope you had your tetanus jabs?'

'Tetanus jabs...for what?'

'This is Merffa, love, you've got to be careful in these parts....typhoid, cholera, hepatitis B, malaria, black plague,' a black man near the door, coughed. 'Sorry...African American plague...lazy fuckers plague, rabies, yellow fever and the worse of all, itchy arse syndrome.'

'No, I haven't,' Dorothy looked shocked, 'what shall I do?

'It should be alright but just don't give anyone a love bite and no back-door action. Anyway, why are you here?'

Terry the dog's ear pricked up. He licked his lips.

'I'm looking for a place that Terry and I will not get into trouble...and....and...'

From out of the kitchen, the chef, dressed like a bad Elvis Presley impersonator appeared holding a wok. He leapt up onto a table and sung, 'If you're looking for trouble...you've came to the right place...If you're...looking...for....'

'Hang on,' Glinda yelled, 'she said, she's not looking for trouble...Bruce fucking Presley fucking Leeeeeeeeeee...now get back in that kitchen.'

'Are you sure? I'm positive she said she was looking for trouble!'

'No, she definitely said, not looking for trouble.'

'Can I sing it anyway?'

'You do and I will blow your bollocks off.' Glinda pointed the gun at him.

The chef walked back into the kitchen. He reappeared again. 'What about Kung Fu fighting then? Everyone loves that.' He serenaded a pair of lesbians eating their food with only one big spoon. 'Everybody was...Kung...Fu...fighting...'

A few people join in, clapping their hands.

Glinda pulled back the trigger. 'Just get back in that kitchen, Shakin' fucking Stevens and stop jerking off in the curry sauce...again.'

Every one of the customers spat a mouthful of curry onto their tables. Glinda eyeballed each of them in turn until they scooped up every bit and re-ate it.

Dorothy put her head in her hands. 'I ran away see...cos they wanted me to marry Dozy Git, and there was a ten-foot chicken...and they wanted to cut Terry's lipstick off for messing with Miss Slocombe's pussy.'

Glinda smirked to herself. She looked around the room. 'Hang on a minute, am I on candid fuckin' camera here? I am, aint I? You bunch of bastards...where is the camera? Come on...come out.'

Dorothy got up to her feet. Shaking her head. Tears rolled down her cheeks, she muttered, 'no...it's true...so I ran away...but now I wanna go back home to my Aunty Em and Uncle Henry. I miss them. I don't like this place.'

'Well, just fu...fu...go home then, love.'

'But I can't go back the way I came...it was terrible...There were horrible, horrible men...everywhere. Can you help me please, Glinda?'

'I'm too busy love...but you need to go see the wizard.'

'Roy Wood?'

'Of course, it's not Roy fucking Wood...this isn't Christmas Tops of the fucking Pops?'

'Sorry.'

'No...the wizard of Gurnoz.'

'The wizard of Gurnoz!' Dorothy repeated.

'Yeah....it was going to be named the Gurnos but the dull fucking painters from the council couldn't fucking spell it properly.'

'The Gurnos! They couldn't spell the Gurnos.'

'Yeah...the fucking Gurnos.' Glinda looked a little pissed off.

'But where will I find him?'

'Giro-city.'

'Giro-city.'

'Yeah, Giro-fucking city. Now stop repeating everything I fucking say. Are you backward or something?'

The lesbian, with the slightly longer set of sideburns to her lover, piped up, 'Well she did say she was from Bedlinog.'

Everyone laughed and whistled the duelling banjo song.

Dorothy ignored them. 'Giro-city...but how do I get there?'

Glinda winked at her. 'You just follow the yellow piss-stained road.'

'The yellow pissed stained road?'

'Fuck me, here we go again...Yeah, the yellow pissed stained road. It's a road covered in piss,' she glared at Terry the dog, 'and dog shit. But beware...it can be dangerous journey...a warning...don't go anywhere near Gethin Woods.

'Why?'

'Full of doggers...or the toilets by the bus station.'

'Why?'

'Full of druggies...or the Wyndham Arms.'

Everyone in the restaurant made a loud Oooooo'ing sound.

'The Wyndham Arms,' Dorothy muttered.

Glinda moved in close to the girl's face. 'Full of lunatics...and whatever you do...don't even look at the Gurnoz club.'

'Oooooooooooooo...Noooooooooooooo,' the punters in the restaurant not only let go of a loud Ooooooooooo'ing sound, but also added a bigger Nooooooooooo at the end of it.

'Why?' asked Dorothy, clutching her dog tight in her arms.

Glinda pulled out a Polaroid photo from her apron and showed it to the girl. The people in the photograph were so ugly they made the creatures in the bar of the film Star Wars look more like the beautiful morons off the TV show, Made in Chelsea. Dorothy shivered. Terry's tongue rolled out of his mouth. Glinda added, 'and that was last year's kid's Christmas party.'

'Oh my...But how am I going to get to giro-city? Someone stole my shoes when I was asleep.'

Glinda looked over her shoulder. She spied the slutty woman in the white dress still slumped over the table. 'Hang on, love.' She bounded over to the sleeping tart and removed her white stilettos. 'Try these on.'

Dorothy stepped into the shoes with ease. 'Perfect...but will she mind?

Glinda laughed. 'Don't worry about the old Wicked Bitch of Planning...she's a right pisshead...been in Spoons all afternoon with the rest of the councillors,' Glinda made hand gestures, '"Business Meeting", she won't remember fuck all in the morning...but watch out for her sister. The Wicked Bitch of the Council...she's like Hitler with lipstick, and two big hairy balls.'

This time an Arrrggghhhhhhhhhhhhh sound rose up from everyone in the place.

'She sounds nasty. Can't you come with me, Glinda?'

The waitress picked her nose and flicked it at the wall. It stuck. 'One hundred and fuckin' eighty.' She danced around the room. Her apron over her head like a dull footballer who just scored a goal. 'Sorry, love,' she settled back down, 'I've got to go make a new batch of spring rolls in a minute.'

From out of the kitchen, the high-pitched drone of the chorus of Kung Fu Fighting drafted out.

'I fuckin' warned that twatting cook,' Glinda marched away and disappeared. Seconds later, a single gunshot rang out.

Everyone in the placed scrambled out into the High Street.

Chapter 5
HIGH

As the night closed in, Dorothy with Terry held firmly in her arms tried to doze off in the piss smelling subway near the flats at the far end of the town. The wind blew bitterly cold as the two friend's cwtched up together under a cardboard box. It proved to be a restless exercise. The silence of the night was often pierced by the frequent sound of police sirens and numerous fights breaking out outside Chang's fish shop.

Next morning, Dorothy walked up through the deserted High Street. It stood eerily quiet on that Sunday morning. She sidestepped between the smashed beer bottles, half eaten kebabs and rubbish which littered the crazy patterned pavement. She almost slipped over on a pool of blood by a bench. Several human teeth lay in the red liquid. Two heroin addicts sat on the church step trying to get the top off a stolen vinegar bottle. A tramp slept under yesterday's newspapers in a doorway. The tramp's dog, a white bitch, bent over eating the remains of a bag of chips. Terry eyed up the white bitch's tight rear end.

'I wouldn't mind me a piece of that.' He was just about to introduce her to his "little friend" when Dorothy rained on his parade.

'No, no...you don't Romeo,' she said, 'it's cos of you we are in this situation in the first place.'

Terry the dog looked at her in amazement, 'Me....me,' he muttered to himself. Kettle ...black...if you had married Dozy Git and had a few in-bred kids...we would still be in Bedlinog now...so don't go blaming me...Miss Picture-Perfect.'

Oblivious, Dorothy continued her journey. She followed the yellow pissed stained road towards the top end of town leaving the dog barking to itself. Rows and rows of empty shops, boarded up and left for dead by past owners, stared back at her.

Terry caught up with her.

'This looks like a terrible run-down place, Terry. It looks worse than that place called Baghdad after a bombing raid.'

She stared at the yellow road full of potholes. It branched off in two directions. She looked one way then the other.

'Follow the yellow piss stained road Glinda said,' Dorothy looked puzzled, 'now which way do we go, Terry? Back down that way, past the tramp in the doorway with that dog?' Terry's lipstick popped out. 'Or across the bridge where that strange woman is offering something called blow jobs for a fiver?'

His both eyebrows perked up. 'Oooohh, that sounds even better,' he panted, his sex pistol throbbing like a plump, ripe pimple on the snotty nose of a snotty teenager.

Still looking confused, Dorothy slumped down near a big bronze statue of a man who had been famous for inventing something in 1854 that no one in the town could remember what it was. A traffic cone lodged on the statue's head and TWWAT (with two W's) sprayed on his forehead proved that no one even cared.

A man in a shirt and tie and fancy shoes stopped beside the girl. He eyed her up for a good minute. 'You look like you could do with some cash.' He undid his fly and added, 'how about a tenner for a quick lick?'

'I am not doing that,' protested Dorothy.

'I'm talking to the dog,' the man clarified.

Dorothy looked at Terry and shrugged. 'Well, we could do with the money, Terry.'

'Don't you dare, "we could do with the money, Terry," me,' the dog barked. 'Who do you think I am? George fuckin' Michael?' The dog turned to the man. 'And you, you little pervert...come here...I'll show you a lick now.' With teeth snarling Terry chased the man down the passageway.

Dorothy leant on a wall in the shadows of the old general hospital. 'I only want to get to Giro City,' she murmured, 'but I don't know which way to go.'

'I wouldn't go that way...its freaky maaaan,' a gruff sounding voice rose from behind a badly maintained hedge.

'Who said that?'

Bob, the fortysomething ex-roadie and now full-time dope smoker, got up from his settee which was neatly positioned in the overgrown front garden of an abandoned house. Around him lay a bottle of cider, a bag of stash and a half-eaten pack of Hobnob biscuits, (the chocolate coated ones of course). Without her noticing him, he staggered up behind Dorothy and took her arm. He pointed it in the other direction. 'And that way is even freakier.'

Dorothy turned to face the ponytailed hippy.

She screamed.

Bob screamed.

Dorothy screamed again, only louder.

Bob screamed again, only louder and more girly than the girl.

Terry came running to her rescue. He barked and snapped at the hippies open toe sandals.

'What're you screaming for?' Bob cried, while kicking out at the savage mutt. 'Well? Get off me, Deputy Dawg.'

Dorothy stood clutching her heart in silence. Eventually, she blurted out, 'you scared me.'

'Did I?' She nodded. He continued, 'Oh I'm sorry, I'm a bit out of it see...anyway...if I was you...I'd stay right here and have a toke on this.' He offered her his half smoked joint.

She shook her head. 'No thank you, I don't smoke. By the way, which way is giro-city?'

He lay back on the settee. His eyes closed. He drifted back off into a daze. 'What?'

'Giro-city?'

'Who me?'

'Yes, you...are you stupid or something?'

'No, I'm not stupid...I'm just stoned maaaannnn. I have a master's degree in life...and agriculture.' He looked at his joint and giggled.

Dorothy looked him up and down suspiciously. 'Is that what you do for a living then?'

'What?'

'You know...what you do for work?'

Bob gripped the worn-out arms of the red PVC settee to steady himself. 'Wor...wor...wor...wor,' he couldn't get the word out, 'me...I haven't wo...wo...wor...that since...since...I was your age...bard bad see...and issues...lots of tissues...issues.' He puffed on the joint. The smoke exhaled from his ears.

'You haven't got a job?'

'No! I haven't got a jjj...jjjjo...jjjjjjooooo...one of them things. My existence is the only jjjjjo...jjjjjooooo...thing I need.'

Terry barked like Lassie in the old movies. Dorothy pulled the creature up to her ear. 'What's that Terry...if he hasn't got a job, how can he afford drugs, drink and high-quality biscuits?'

'Oh...oh,' Bob paced about. 'I get a bit of money from the social...and I used to do a bit of roadying until my back went. So, tell your Mutt there...that there are a lot of people in Merthyr without Jobs...that do an awful lot of working. Ain't that right boys? He saluted a gang of men in high Viz railway jackets shuffling into a van.

'Mind your own c█ting business, junkie,' one of the men shouted as their van drove away on four bald tyres.

60

'We haven't really met properly, have we?' Dorothy held out her hand and Terry's paw. 'I'm Dorothy and this is Terry.

Bob looked at the creature. 'Terry...looks more like a Tonto to me......or Toto, I went on tour with them in the eighties, what a laugh, talk about sex, drugs and sausage rolls...good days...good old days.'

'No...it's Terry...Terry the dog...look it says Terry on his collar. How much of that stuff do you smoke?'

'Only a couple of joints now and again.' He picked up the dog. 'And it's important that I keep smoking it see. Cos to be the part of Bob, I must live the part of Bob. To be Bob, or not to be Bob? That is the question.' He tried to put the joint in the dog's mouth.

'No,' Dorothy grabbed the dog back out of his arms. 'So, your name is Bob.'

'It's Robert Dope...sorry, Hope...but everyone calls me Bob.'

She offered her hand again. 'Nice to meet you Bob...Now let's get you up.'

'Oh, I don't know about that...I'm not feeling well at all...and Jeremy Kyle's on now in a minute.'

Dorothy tried her best to pull the older man up.

'Oh...oh...watch the clobber...Rossi from Quo gave me this waistcoat...and these jeans.' He did a little twirl. 'Clearly, he didn't actually give them to me...I borrowed them...but you know what they say.' He stopped talking; his eyes stared up at the sky.

'No...what do they say?'

'What?'

'What do they say?'

'Fuck knows...it's not important.'

'Oh ok...now come on get up.'

'Get off me...I've got nothing to get up for.'

'Of course, you have.'

'Name one thing?'

Dorothy pulled at his sleeve with all her might. 'Your self-respect.'

Bob leapt to his feet as if the postman had just popped his giro through the letterbox. Dorothy lost her grip. She fell back on to the grass. 'Don't make me laugh,' he held his finger in the air to make a point, 'self-respect...the socials put me on a zero-hour contract.'

He helped her up. 'What does that mean...zero hours?'

'Means I'm a slave...Kunta Kinta Bob.' He stared off into the distance for a few seconds. He snapped back to reality. 'So, I'm going to sit here...and...' Bob slumped back down. He puffed hard on the joint. He dozed off. The lit end of the joint burnt a hole in his scruffy jeans. He jumped.

'Come on...let's get you up.' She pulled him to his feet. 'Maybe we can see if you can get a job.'

'A jjjj...jjjjo...jjjjoooo.' She slapped his face. 'A joooooooob...ok, but hang on now, love...I need another spliff.'

'Oh no you don't...keep walking...keep moving.'

Bob's legs felt like jelly. He stood unsteady on his feet. He walked a few strides but fell head over tit over the settee, landing next to some fresh dog poop. He growled at Terry. 'But I'm too much of a loser.' The pot-head clambered back up on to his feet.

'There must be something you can do?' prompted Dorothy.

Munching on a biscuit, Bob paced about. 'Well...I can...I can...I can roll an eight skinner with one hand while scratching my nuts with the other...look.'

'I'm quite naïve but I guess there's not much call for someone who can roll an eight skinner with one hand, while scratching their nuts with the other.'

Bob stopped dead in his tracks. Her words waved in front of him like a red rag at a bull. He stood on the settee like an MP giving a speech on stage at a conference. 'There used to be in the good old days when everyone loved a good old puff, I was in demand. But now all these bloody youngsters are just cooking up heroin and sniffing cheap cocaine, or crack, ketamine, ecstasy, methadone, meow meow, m-cat, drone, bubbles, bounce...and what's all that planet food about? I took a nose-bag of that the other day. I woke up in the morning and I had a bunch of daffodils growing out of my pooper.' He struck a relative pose.

Dorothy looked at Terry. The dog shrugged his doggy shoulders.

'But imagine what you could do if you did have a job.'

'Why, if I had a jjjjjjooo...jjjjjjjooooob...I would probably,' he kind of sang, 'while away the hours, maybe buy some girl some flowers, and stop being such a slob, and while my wallets bunglin', my mind would be busy hatchin', If I only had a j...j...j...I can't even bloody say it.'

He climbed halfway up a lamppost and continued, 'I'd drink the best champagne, and go up the Richards with Jeff and Lorraine, I'd become such an Uptown snob, I would not be just a nuffin', my head all full of stuffin', there would be no need to go out on the rob. And become known as Bob the j...j...j...Job...And I would definitely get an extension for my little knob.' Bob puffed on his unlit joint, 'if I only had a jooooooooob.'

'Will you shut the fuck up,' a man in a white wife-beater vest screamed from an upstairs window, 'I'm trying to give my Misses one here mun and you are spoiling the mood.'

'I could come up and help if you want,' Bob winked, 'I've heard she likes a couple at a time.'

Terry the dog's ears pricked up. 'I'm not fussed about having sloppy thirds,' he barked.

'You, cheeky fucker.' The man threw a half full bottle of white lightening at him. 'I'll come down there and give you one now.' He slammed the window shut.

'I think we should be off, my dear.' Bob took Dorothy's hand. They marched her up the hill by the side of the old hospital.

Dorothy stopped to catch her breath. 'If you lived in Bedinog...there would be plenty of jobs for you to do.'

'I don't want anything too hard mind,' he talked as they walked up the street.

Dorothy looked up to the heavens. 'Working on the farm...picking apples...milking Roger.'

'Not Roger Moore...don't tell me that?' Bob leaned on a car.

'No...Roger the cow.'

'Thank god for that,' Bob clutched his heart, 'I couldn't cope with another scandal involving a celebrity from the 70's especially Bond...James Bond. So, where's Bedlinog then?

'That's where I live...or lived...And I want to get back there so badly I'm going all the way to Giro-City to get the Wizard of Gurnoz to help me.'

'I luvs Roy Wood me. I did crack...sorry, I had the craic with him one night...I wish it could be Christmas everyday me...Do you think this Wizard would give me a j...j...j...job? Nothing to hard mind...nice office number...start at 11...finish at 2...ish...hour for dinner...a few puff breaks?'

'I couldn't say. But maybe you'd better not. It's dangerous I've been told there's some mad bitch out there.'

He laughed. 'I'm not afraid of a bitch! I've been on tour with Ozzy don't forget, when he was right mental like. I'm not afraid of anything...well except losing my stash.' He held up a big bag of weed. 'Or not getting my giro. But I really wanna get a jjjjjjjoooob now. Can I come? I won't be any trouble, because I don't eat much...unless I have the munchies on....and I won't try to manage things, because I'm always stoned.'

'Why, of course you can. To Gurnoz!'

Bob took a long, slow drag on his joint. 'To Gurnoz!'

Dorothy started to skip and sing. 'We're off to see the Wizard...the Wonderful Wizard of Gurn...OZ.'

Bob looked at her as if she'd gone mental. 'Never mind that shite...let's see if there's a café open...I need a strong cup of brew and a Kit Kat.'

Chapter 6
WHEELIE BINS

If the Wicked Bitch of the Council had her way the council chamber in the town hall would resemble a torture chamber not a plush office. She fantasized about having all manner of instruments of pain, for her pleasure, around her. Teeth extractors, toe snappers, branding irons and a variety of large, black dildos. She'd have a device to stretch people who needed to be stretched, and a machine to squash people who needed squashing. A bit like JD Sports, but run by the criminally insane.

On the walls, she pictured a line of "trophy" decapitated heads. Stuffed noodles staring out like once proud animals on a hunter's wall. Her "trophies" would be of stupid and reckless idiots who have done stupid things to piss her off over the years.

Pride of place, she pictured, the ugly bonce of the pathetic councillor who for some godforsaken reason decided to reduce the price of parking on the weekends in the town centre to just a pound.

'It will help with the shop trade in the town centre,' he announced in the meeting a few years ago.

At that time, the Wicked Bitch had just been a junior clerk working in finance. Even though she wanted to object to the ridiculous suggestion, she didn't have the authority or the power. The motion got carried. Parking charges went from £6 per day to only a quid. 'Only a fuckin' quid,' the Wicked Bitch was still tamping even up to this day. How could her colleagues be so ludicrous? If she had her way, she would have doubled the cost of parking. 'Let the mean, lazy bastards pay more, the lot of them.'

That changed as soon as she got the top job. Not only did she hike the parking prices up straight away, she also ensured the councillor. who proposed the change. got sacked. And just to prove a point and send out a strong message, she had the bloke's car burnt out. No one even suggested a price reduction again.

Next to him, she'd display the odd-shaped craniums of the Mayor and his bloody wife. 'Common as muck they are. The both of them,' she often yelled out in meetings when their names got mentioned. 'For fuck sake, he worked on the assembly line in Hoovers before he got elected, and she worked in Penydarren Fish Shop. She still smells of cod. Little bit of power and he thinks he's fucking Pablo Escobar and the way she struts around Castle Bingo, she thinks she's fuckin' Madonna, but with more fucking wrinkles.'

Lastly, on the long wall opposite her window she would leave space entirely for all the heads of the members of the last Labour council. For some stupid reason, those idiots agreed en-mass to erect bronze statues of boxers around the town.

'Boxers for fuck sake,' she said to herself, 'Eddie Thomas, Jonny Owen, not even the actor, the smaller one with the big ears, and Howard Windmill or whatever his name was. Honoured for punching heads in. What type of example does that give to the youth of this town?' Go out and smash someone and get awarded for it...ridiculous.'

This town and its mentality infuriated her at times. 'Power is wasted on the fucking stupid,' she said on more than one occasion, 'and those councillors were the dullest of the fuckin' dull.'

Her vision was clear. There would be a bronzed statue of her in the centre of the precinct. Over 12-foot-tall enclosed in a glass case so the pigeons couldn't shite on it or drunken idiots couldn't place traffic cones on her head at weekends and write the word "Twat" on her forehead. She even considered hiring a sniper, with a licence to kill, to watch over it from the building opposite.

With that image fixed in her mind, she reclined back in her expensive Italian leather chair. Her black, thigh high boots rested on her desk. On his knees, next to her, her personal gimp panted like a well-behaved dog. He handed the phone to his master. The Wicked Bitch let the person on the other end talk for a few seconds. Her face turning a deeper shade of red with every word. She interrupted by yelling down the receiver. 'I don't fuckin' care. I want them closed.'

The voice on the other end quietly muttered, 'but Wicked Bitch...are you sure?'

'Look you idiot, how many people in this town read?'

Silence.

'Well?'

'Quite a few I imagine.'

'Yeah,' the Wicked Bitch growled, 'if you include The Hustler, page 3 of The Sun and the Racing Post. Most of these people in this fuckin' town would struggle with series two of Dick and fucking Dora....so, I want the libraries closed...understand?'

There was another brief pause. 'But when?'

'Monday.'

'But...but...Monday is World Book Day and we have lots of activities planned with the kids.'

'I don't give a flying fuck...close them, close them or |I'll close you!' She slammed the receiver down. Spit dribbled down her chin.

The gimp clambered up her leg and licked the gob off.

'Get off me, you cretin.' She slapped him out of the way. She glanced up at the large portrait of Margret Thatcher hanging with pride on the wall behind her desk. 'I'll show you Queen Maggie...I will be more powerful than you one day...wait and see.'

A knock on the door broke her concentration. She clicked her fingers, the gimp shuffled across the carpet on all fours and hid in the small, silver box near the water fountain. Another knock. She purposely didn't answer. One of her rules of management was to always let them wait, let them stew in their own juices, or their own shit with a bit of luck. Her other rules consisted of words like bully the fuckers, shout at the bastards and eliminate as many of the dull twats as she could. Her philosophy was straight out of the Goebbels's book of command and control.

Another knock. She waited, a smirk building on her face.

'Enter,' she finally bellowed.

Three men skulked in to the room in cheap polyester suits. Nervously, they sat down around the table. The Wicked Bitch wandered behind them. 'Did I tell you to sit?" she cried.

The men all shot back up to their feet.

'Sit,' she quietly hissed in one of the men's ears.

They did what she instructed.

She paced behind them, menacingly. Under their suits, the men's armpits filled up with sweat. Fear crawled over their skin like some horrible earwig who hadn't shaved his legs for a month and nestled somewhere in the men's underpants.

'Let's get this bloody thing over with,' she instructed.

'Ok,' the man wearing the Disney character tie's voice shook in terror, 'first item on our Town Hall's budget meeting is...' He didn't finish his sentence.

'Town Halls slashing meeting you mean.' She laughed. They joined her. She whacked the table with her long black truncheon that had been strapped to her leg. Her face transformed. 'Well I hope it's what you mean.'

The bald man on the left piped up, 'I've slashed the hospital budget.'

'By how much?' the Wicked Bitch snarled. The others glanced slyly across at him. He gulped. His Adam's apple protruded so much it looked like he had swallowed a medium sized stoat wearing a top hat. '45...percent.'

'Not bad...not bad at all.' The man let go of a sigh. He wiped the beads of warm sweat away from his brow. The man next to him tapped his colleague's knee in congratulations. 'BUT I WANT MORE,' the bitch yelled, 'another 20%!'

The councillor in charge of environment and refuge, chipped up sternly. 'Ok, boss, I've reduced the size of their wheelie bins.'

'How small are they?' she glared at him, suspicion written all over her face.

'About this size.' He used his hands to indicate the new dimensions.

'Not small enough...I want them smaller and...and let me throw this at you and see if it sticks.' Perspiration dripped down the man's head onto his lap. 'How about if we only collect the bins every, let's say, six weeks instead of every week.'

'Six weeks? Collect the bins every six weeks?'

'Yeah...six fucking weeks...do you have a problem with it?'

The man shook his head. He wrote the words, six weeks, in large letters onto his note pad. Inwardly, he wasn't a happy bunny. He knew there would be uproar and he would take the blunt end of the abuse, yet again.

Disney character tie man put his hand up. 'I've reduced the town's bus service to one bus a day.' He left a pause, 'and that,' another pause, 'doesn't even stop anywhere.'

'Splendid. What about these awful schools?'

The councillor in charge of environment and refuge shook his head. 'But Wicked Bitch...smaller wheelie bins...like the size of a dwarf?'

'What?'

'The wheelie bins...small...like really small...like dwarf size? '

'I don't care if they are the same size as Alan the fuckin' midget. Schools?'

71

The bald man jumped in. 'we've sacked half the teachers.'

The Wicked Bitch smacked the truncheon into the palm of her hand. 'Half...only half. I want the school's budget slashed...slashed...slashed...and talking of schools...I want the buses that transport those awful kids to school stopped immediately.'

'But how will the children get to school?' he said without realising the words had escaped out of his mouth.

'Oh yes I forgot. How will they get to school? Let me think.' She giggled. One of her infamous schoolgirl giggles. To the people who had worked for her for a while, they knew her giggle was far worse than her bark, but not her bite. At least, when she yelled and screamed they were fully aware of where she was coming from. When she let go of one of her schoolgirls giggles it was like a shark smirking on seeing someone's leg dangling off an airbed as it skimmed through the water. They all recognised, the bite was coming.

The bald man did his own version of the giggle. He was quite new and didn't fully understand the dangerous water he found himself swimming in. The others just sat there, staring at their shoes. In their minds, the scary music from Jaws played out. The Bitch participated for a full twenty seconds. Giggle...another giggle...then....

BANG!

She smashed the truncheon down hard on the oak table. 'I don't give a fuck. Let the fat, lazy, McDonald eating bastards walk. What about meals on wheels?'

'Shut down,' said Disney character tie man.

'Good job. Car parking?

They glanced at the bald man again. He muttered. 'I've increased the charges by 200%...and as per your instructions, I issued the traffic wardens with Taser guns.'

'Excellent...I fucking loves traffic wardens. Good god, I'm actually feeling quite horny.' She lightly squeezed her tit. A noise like a clown's horn escaped from inside the silver box on the other side of the room. The men looked at the chest, then at each other.

Her features changed. A snarl lit up her face. 'What about that drug rehabilitation centre up in the Gurnoz...run by that...that.' She spat on the floor, 'that goody-two shoes?' She scrutinised every one of them in turn

They all stared down at the carpet

'WELL?'

'But we can't close it, Wicked Bitch,' the bald man was the only one brave enough to say anything, 'we have a massive drug problem in the town...it's out of control.'

'I know it is...who do you think sells them all the drugs in the first place? Those drugs pay for my holiday flat in Malaga...so I want it closed.'

'But what will happen to all the poor addicts?'

'It starts with "I don't care" and ends in "flying fuck". So, get it sorted or else.'

The councillor in charge of the environment and refuge still had a concern 'But Wicked Bitch...if we make the bins, dwarf size, they won't be able to store half a week's worth of rubbish never mind six...'

The blow of the truncheon to his exposed head caused a sickening thud. He was out cold before his head hit the oak table top. She whacked him several more times for good luck.

'I don't care about fuckin' wheelie bins...I want that drug place closed...I want it burned to the ground and that wizard hung from the nearest lamppost by his nuts.' The two other men grabbed their own crown jewels. 'Now get out.' The two men got up and walked towards the door. 'And take this fucking idiot with you.'

They started to drag the unconscious man out. 'What shall we do with him?' one of the men asked.

'I don't care.' She smirked. 'Oh, hang on, I know...put him in a fucking wheelie bin until he comes around.' She cackled to herself. 'Then tell him he's fuckin' fired.'

They left just as the Wicked Bitch's youngest sister staggered in, barefooted, holding a bottle of gin.

'Hey Sis...how's planning going?' the Wicked Bitch tutted as she cleaned a large amount of white powder from her sister's nose. 'For fuck sake, Sis...you ain't Danielle Westbrook you know.'

'But I'm stressed.' The sister made a face as if she was having some form of drug related stroke. Which considering the number of drugs and booze she got through daily, wouldn't have been a surprise. She was the original IT girl, the party animal. While the Wicked Bitch of the Council had spent most of her life scheming and planning her way to the top, her younger, prettier sister had just gone about enjoying life. She'd been expelled from every school and college she had ever attended. Her record for holding down a job was a day shy of two weeks. She only got the role of Bitch of Planning after her sister promised her dying grandmother she would look out for her. She was completely out of her depth. However, she loved the role as due to the amount of red tape in the planning process there was never anything to do, well unless the Wicked Bitch wanted something done. Then her sister would simply delegate it to someone in the department and go off for a liquid lunch in one of the nearest boozers.

'That Mayor's a twat,' the sister spat her words, 'he's refusing to agree for our pay-as-you-cum brothel in the old primary school.'

'We'll see about that.' The Wicked Bitch pointed to the floor. 'Hey, where's my shoes?'

'What shoes?' the woman screwed up her face.

'You know what shoes. My brand-new white Julien MacDonald 'essential' Merffa stilettoes.' She held up a box with the designer's face on it holding a white shoe. She bowed to it.

'Oh...em shoes...some girl nicked them off me in Hing Hongs.'

The Wicked Bitch counted to ten. 'How the hell could some girl pinch MY shoes off YOUR feet while you were in a Chinese restaurant? Were you pissed again?

'No...honest. Well I just had one...you know...to take the edge off.'

'I'll take the fucking edge off you in a minute.' She held up her truncheon.

'But she had a gun, sis.'

'A gun, you say.'

'Yeah...a Cornetto 69 I think it was, and she had a dog. A fucking big dog...fucking huge....it had a saddle and all...and...and...'

'I'll dog her. I want those shoes back. They are important to me. They are one of a kind. Now come on...let's go and sort that Mayor and his fucking wife out.' The Wicked Bitch turned and headed to the big oak door.

'But...I need some pills first.' The Bitch of Planning stood eyes wide like the last, lonely puppy dog in a pet shop at Christmas. 'Please?'

'For god sake...top drawer...but just take two...TWO, I said.'

Chapter 7

LECH WALESA

The one remaining rusty, tatty, old gate leading into the discarded playground hung on a single hinge like a rock climber hanging one handed on the side of a cliff. Knee high grass threatened to completely overrun the last few metres of bare concrete flooring. Spray can graffiti on the broken equipment was the only sign that life existed in this part of the estate. It looked like a ghost-park. The swings had long lost their swing. The merry-go-round lay rusty and jammed and refused to budge.

Dorothy and Bob walked passed the weather-beaten plaque at the entrance to the park gates which stated, for anyone that cared, that 'this fully equipped and newly designed modern park was proudly opened by Mayor William Sticks on March 11th 1968.'

'Yeah...I done 'em all see...Sabbath...Zeppelin...Floyd. Em were the days.' Bob puffed on a freshly rolled joint. He leant against the rocking horse which hadn't rocked and rolled in anger for many a long year.

'What's happened here?' Dorothy asked, 'what a mess?'

'Life,' Bob replied, 'just life.'

'What are you doing now?' She looked in disgust as he stood rifling through a manky looking rubbish bin.

'I've got the munchies...right on me.' He picked a decomposed rat from out of the bin by its tail. He licked his lips. 'It ain't a Bombay Bad Boy pot noodle, but I guess it will do.'

'You can't eat that?'

'I've eaten worse. Should have seen the shite we ate in Japan with the boys from Whitesnake. Em were dark days, let me tell you, very dark indeed.'

'Oh...Oh,' an angry voice shouted. 'I'm saving that for my supper, hippy boy.' A scruffy looking woman lay out on a park bench. Next to her, a Tesco shopping trolley full of crappy stuff.

'Oh, sorry mister...we didn't know,' Dorothy muttered.

'You, cheeky git. I'm a woman.'

Bob doubled over laughing. 'Now that dude does not look like a lady.' He winked at Dorothy, 'Aerosmith 1992...Wembley Stadium...the best drugs I've ever had. Now 'em dudes can party, let me tell you.'

Baglady gobbed on the floor. 'Oh, look who's talking...its Cheech, or is it fucking Chong? I can never remember.'

'I've actually met them once...'

'Shut it Hippy boy. I don't care and put my fuckin' dinner back' she groaned out in pain as she tried to get up. 'Hey you, girlie...come here and giz me a drop of me white lightening.'

Dorothy picked up the half empty cider bottle. Unscrewing the top, she leant in to offer the old woman a sip. She nearly heaved as the intense aroma from the woman's body odour attacked her nostrils. Alcohol mixed with the stench of the Baglady's armpits smelt worse than Uncle Henry's breath. She put her hand to her nose.

Stepping back, Dorothy studied the old woman's face as she struggled to pour the cider into her rancid mouth. Every line on the woman's face could probably tell its own story of angst and suffering. Years and years of dirt and depression engrained into every pore on the poor street woman's complexion. Yet, Dorothy saw something behind the mud pack of daily life splattered on the woman's hardened features. She

78

saw something in her eyes, a hidden goodness to her. A kind and considerate person. A person who would go out of her way to help people. Dorothy smiled at her.

'For fuck sake,' the Baglady snatched the drink off the girl 'you ain't oiling me like the fucking tin man. Are you backward or something?' She gulped down the cider before throwing the plastic container back into her shopping trolley.

'She is from Bedlinog,' Bob laughed.

'Enough said. Have you married your first cousin yet?' the Baglady blew her nose into the sleeve of her dirty, old coat. She scrutinised the contents.

'No!' Dorothy folded her arms and added quietly, 'he's too weird.'

'So, happy for you…now bugger off.'

'That's not very nice. We're only trying to help,' Dorothy protested.

'I don't want your help…piss off I said.'

'That's very rude.'

'Look love…Five years ago my husband passed away.' She waited for a glimmer of sympathy. It didn't materialise. 'Did you hear me then? Or are you deaf as well as fucking thick. I said five years ago my husband Ernie passed away.'

'Oh, I'm so sorry to hear that,' Dorothy said.

Behind them, leaning on the rocking horse, Bob nodded his head in agreement. 'Tragic,' he muttered.

'Don't fecking patronize me, you bunch of in-breds.' She glared at them both in turn. 'Anyway, he died and then the council stopped my allowance, threw me out of my house onto the street. I lived in a wheelie bin for a while, until they made them so small I couldn't get in it. I've been living rough ever since.'

'That's terrible.'

'I know it is, girlie.' Snatching the rat off Bob, she stuffed it in her pocket. 'Now both of you, and that mutt, go and take a long walk on the A470 in the fucking dark.'

'You're so heartless,' Dorothy looked shocked.

'Heartless? Heartless? How would you feel living on the streets without a roof over your head?

'Well, why don't you try and get a house.'

Baglady laughed. A lump of phlegm caught deep down in her throat. 'Urrrggghhhhh,' she coughed. The green gob sailed through the air. It landed with a splat on Terry's back. The dog raced around in horror, rolling around on the grass trying to dislodge the green, slimy monster. Baglady continued, 'a house...around here...it ain't as easy as that, love.'

'But why? I've seen lots of boarded up houses and shops around,' Dorothy suggested.

'Let me tell you why now, Girlie.' The woman coughed again. Everyone ducked out of the way. Baglady started to half-spoke, half-sang. 'When a woman as got a kettle, be it plastic or be it metal, She shouldn't be a louse, Just because I'm presumin', That I could be kind-a human, If I only had a house.' The old hobo hobbled around using the shopping trolley as support. Bob held his nose due to the smell.

'It's like Phantom of the fuckin' opera,' Terry the dog barked to himself yet again.

Baglady continued, 'I'd be tender...I'd be gentle, And awful sentimental, I wouldn't even eat a mouse, or a rat, I'd have a fridge full of Pepsi max, And I would even pay the bedroom tax...If I only had a house. Ooooohhhhhhhh,' she winced in pain and rubbed the base of her spine. 'But they won't give me a house,' she crocked.

Dorothy helped her back to the bench. 'Do you want another drink?' she handed her the bottle from out of the shopping trolley.

'Yep...now go away and stop filling my head full of nonsense about getting a nice, four-bedroom home, with a garden with a fit

Mexican gardener called Ramone,' Baglady snarled at Terry the dog. 'Ouch!' her back stiffened up again.

Several yards away, a black limo pulled ominously up beside the park fence. The window slowly rolled down. The Wicked Bitch of the Council, dressed from head to toe in a black cat suit with thigh high leather boots, listened intently to the conversation taking place. No one noticed her.

'Oh, oh, are you, all right?' Dorothy held out her hand to the Baglady.

'I'm been sleeping rough for too many years. I'm a little rusty.'

'Hey, I have an idea.' She smiled, 'me and Bob, there...'

'Who me?' Bob's eyes rolled about in his dope-filled head.

Dorothy continued, 'Yes, Bob...see we were just wondering why you couldn't come to Giro-City with us to ask the Wizard of Gurnoz for help. Maybe he can get you a house.'

Baglady turned to face the girl. 'Giro City? Me...Baglady in a house?'

'Yeah,' Bob chipped in, 'with a bloody, big, sheep dip.'

The empty cider bottle bounced off his head. 'Shut it Hippy.'

Dorothy paced about. 'Yes, be quiet Bob. But, Baglady, it's worth a try and it would be miles better than living on the street.'

Baglady thought for a moment. A grin replaced her scowl, but soon slipped off her chops again. 'Well, suppose the Wizard is like the rest of the tossers in the council and wouldn't give me one?'

'Oh, but he will! He must! We've come such a long way already. Bob wants a job.'

'Oh...oh.' The hippy staggered unsteadily on his feet. 'Will you stop telling people that? A little fiddle will do me.'

Dorothy ignored him. 'You want a house, and I just want to go back home.'

'Haaaaa...Haaaaaaa...Haaaaaaaaa,' the loud, evil chuckle of the Witch Bitch made them all turn around. The Bitch strolled slowly towards them through the gates, clapping her hands for affect. 'You can't be serious,' she chuckled, 'a job, a house, free travel. You don't look like Polish immigrants.'

'Lech Walesa,' muttered Bob.

'Who's that?' Dorothy replied.

Bob put his arm around the girl's shoulder. 'See, he was a Polish trade unionist in the...'

'No,' Baglady wrestled the situation back. 'It's the Wicked Bitch of the Council...she was the one who threw me out of my house.'

'Oh yeah,' Bob realised his mistake, 'and she was the one who shut down my mate's cannabis factory up in his attic. I was going to be a quality inspector there...honest.'

A woman walking past pushing a pram yelled out, 'And she was the one who sent the troops into Swansea Road looking for weapons of mass destruction.'

Suddenly, a man dressed in women's clothes stepped out from behind a row of trees. 'And she was the one who dressed me up as a woman and made me walk around the woods like this.' Everyone looked at the man in the ginger wig. He walked in front of them. 'Honest...I don't like dressing in woman's clothes...I don't...I'm married with three kids...she did it...she did.' There was a very awkward silence. 'Oh, bollocks to the lot of you.' In high heels, he disappeared back into the woods, fixing his wig to his head.

'Hey, you...girl,' the Wicked Bitch snarled, 'those are my shoes.' Her long, bony fingers aimed at her target.

'These?'

'Yes...and I want them back, this instant.' The evil woman stepped forward, hands outstretched.

Baglady held up a kettle. 'Leave her be...Bitch...or I will.'

'Oh...you're a little firm, are you?' the Witched Bitch's one eyebrow pointed up to the sky, 'like Russian football hooligans.'

'No...worse. We're like the Valley Commandos on Strongbow.'

'Oh, bloody hell,' the Bitch pretended to shiver, 'I'm shitting myself here.' She went serious again. 'We'll see about that.'

Bob tried to put on a brave face. 'Don't worry about her Dorothy...she can't do anything to us.' He quickly stepped back behind the Baglady.

'Hey Bob.' The Wicked Bitch held up a piece of paper the size of a small envelope, 'do you recognise this?'

Without stepping forward, Bob squirted his eyes. 'From where I'm standing, it looks like a giro.'

The cackle from the Wicked Bitch caused birds to fly from the trees. 'Yes, you are perfectly correct...but it's not just any old giro. It's your last giro.'

'Mine.' He walked towards her.

'Yes...and if I'm not mistake, which I'm not, it's your...it's your...last giro. No more invalidity benefits for you.' The malicious lady smirked as she ripped the giro into a hundred pieces.

Bob fell to his knees in slow motion. His scream pierced the air, 'Noooooooooooo.' He scampered around on all fours trying to put all the pieces together.

Wicked Bitch spun around to face the Baglady, 'Hey you...disgusting creature,' she rummaged around in her bag. She pulled out a human skull, 'recognise this?'

'No.'

Wicked Bitch looked at the skull. 'Sorry, wrong one.' She pulled another one out of bag. Printed on the head of this skull were the words. 'The skull of Baglady's husband.'

'Yes,' Baglady cried. 'That's my Ernie...My husband...You, Wicked, Wicked Bitch.'

'That's my name...don't wear it out.' Wicked Bitch threw the skull to the old hobo.

Full of passion, Baglady kissed the skull with all her might. Her long, hairy, pink tongue lost deep inside the mouth of her dead husband.

83

The Wicked Bitch turned to Dorothy. Her eyes burning into the girl's skin. 'And as for you, my little....' Dorothy stood shaking, her dog held firmly in her hands, 'Dorothy, you will never get to see the wizard...and you will never...ever get back to Bedlinog.' The Wicked Bitch laughed and laughed. 'It will be the whore house for you. You will be my little crack whore.'

BANG!

From nowhere, an enormous bang sounded followed by a dense puff of black smoke. When it cleared, the Wicked Bitch and her car had disappeared.

'Fuck me,' the Baglady muttered, 'she's like an evil Paul Daniels.'

'I wouldn't have liked her to have been her tour manager back in the day,' Bob clambered to his feet. He pulled another joint out of the secret pocket in his leather waistcoat. 'She's worse than Charlotte Church's mother...now there's one tough motherfucker, let me tell you.'

They both heard the sobbing at the same time. Dorothy sat on the grass, crying the rain.

Bob reacted first. He staggered over and plonked himself down next to the girl. 'Giro or no giro, Dorothy I'll help you to see the wizard.'

'For the first time ever, I kinda agree with him,' the Baglady added, 'home or no home...I'm going to get you sorted...I hate that bitch.'

Dorothy dried her eyes, 'But she's so wicked, I don't think you two should come with me because you'll get into more trouble.'

'Never mind her my little mirco-dot,' Bob nudged her, 'there must be something we can do.'

'But she's the head of the council...and she's very horrible and nasty.' Tears rolled done the girl's cheeks.

No one spoke. They sat about having a think. Bob rolled a joint. Baglady nudged him. 'What?' he said, 'it helps me think.'

He took a long tote. His eyes came alive. 'Well,' Bob piped up, 'they couldn't have been as horrible and as nasty as Motley Crew on their tour of Japan in 86. Have you even seen what snorting sushi can do to a man...trust me, you never want to either?'

'And the point of your fucking story is, Hippy boy?' screamed Baglady.

'Hum...hummmm...never snort fish.'

'You fucking idiot.'

Dorothy sobbed again.

'Ok...ok,' said Bob, 'I know, talking of mirco-dots...I could spike her coffee with acid...that will fuck her up.'

'That's more like it,' Baglady grinned. 'Yeah...and I could sit on her doorstep...oh sorry, I'm losing it...I could shit on her doorstep in the town hall and run away.'

Dorothy laughed. 'Oh, you're the best friends anybody ever had! And it's funny, but I feel as if I've known you all my life. But I couldn't have, could I?' Bob and Baglady looked at each other. Bob made a sign to suggest the girl was around the bend. 'I guess it doesn't matter anyway. We know each other now, don't we? To Gurnoz!' Dorothy jumped up to her feet. 'Come on...she's not going to stop us.' She grabbed Bob and Baglady under each arm. 'Come on...sing with me...We've off to see the wizard...the wonder wizard of Gurnoz. We hear he is a whiz of a Wiz, If ever a Wiz there was...OZ, If ever, oh ever a Wiz there was...the wiz is ....'

Baglady turned to Bob, 'You haven't given her a puff of that green shit, have you? She's gone fucking mental.'

Bob shook his head. 'No, she's does this all the time. I think she thinks she's Bonny fucking Langford.'

'In that case, give me a puff of that fuckin' stuff,' Baglady held out her hand.

Chapter 8

STRANGEWAYS

'What's that noise?' Dorothy looked back and forth.

The forest they found themselves walking through was darker and creepier than the midget off the Singing, Ringing Tree. *(and for anyone who saw the programme in the 70's, he was right fuckin' scary. Even scarier than the child-catcher from Shitty, Shitty, Bang, Bang).*

The daylight had disappeared behind the mountain. Leaving the shadows to came out too play, along with some other right old weirdos.

'What noise?' Bob asked.

'That slurping noise. Sounds like someone's milking old Roger?'

'Not Roger fucking Moore?' Baglady stopped in her tracks, 'don't tell me that now...I'm only just getting over Rolf and his horny paint brush.'

'No,' laughed Bob, 'Roger is a cow...apparently. She had me on that one and all.'

'Schhhhhhh...Listen,' Dorothy grabbed Baglady's arm.

They stopped. Bob was first to speak, 'to be honest girl, it does sound like someone milking a cow or maybe someone slurping on a long, ice cold lolly pop.'

'Probably, doggers,' replied Baglady, 'and they're probably milking something or other. These woods are teaming with them.'

'Glinda mentioned them to me. I didn't understand. Are they people who like dogs then?'

'Amongst other things.' Baglady and Bob nudged each other.

'Oh, I bet they would love Terry then.'

Behind a large bush, the dark figure of an overweight man in a police uniform could be seen. Kneeing down between the Copper's bare legs, a bald man's shiny head bobbed in and out. The policeman moaned and groaned.

'What is that man doing to that poor policeman?' Dorothy asked.

'Well, he's not giving him a fuckin' breathalyser sample,' Baglady laughed.

'OOOOOOOOOOOOOOOOOOOOO,' the policeman's whole body shook violently as he knocked on heaven's door. His face frozen in a happy state of glee.

'Oh, PC Jenkins,' Baglady yelled out, 'I'll tell your wife next time I see her in the butchers.'

As quick as mice running through a field of cats, the two men disappeared out of sight.

'I don't like this place!' Dorothy scooped Terry up in her arms. 'It's...its dark and creepy!'

'I know,' Bob said, trying to dislodge a used condom off his sandal without having to touch it, 'and I think it will get darker before it gets any lighter.'

'Jesus, Mary and Joseph...its Confucius, the dopehead, speaking,' Baglady picked up a piece of wood. She placed it in her shopping trolley.

'I'm only saying maaaaaaaan...respect the light, ain't it.'

'Well don't...you're talking shite...again.'

Dorothy gripped Terry closed to her chest. 'Do you suppose we'll meet any wild creatures?'

'Wild...they'll be bloody tamping,' joked Bob, slapping his thigh in amusement.

Baglady's reply proved to be more serious. 'Yeah, probably.'

'W...w...what type of creatures?' Dorothy stared at her.

'Mostly, smackheads,' muttered Baglady.

Bob joined in, 'and gangsters.'

'And whores,' Baglady grappled hard to get the sentence back.

Dorothy looked at them. 'Smackheads!'

'And gangsters?' added Bob.

'And whores,' Bagllady grunted.

They walked on the path leading from the woods into a field.

'Smackheads, and gangsters, and whores!' they all repeated.

'Oh, my!' Dorothy added at the end.

'Smackheads, and gangsters, and whores!'

'Oh, my!'

'Smackheads, and gangsters, and whores!'

'Oh, my!'

'Smackheads, and gangsters, and whores!'

'Oh, my!'

They walked faster and faster. All of a sudden, from behind a tree, a loud cry engulfed them. They all grabbed around each other. The smell of Baglady's clothes was too much for Bob. He broke the bond.

'What sort of creature is that?' Dorothy asked.

'I'm not sure,' said Baglady, 'but it sounded like a fuckin' big one!'

'D-d-d-don't be fr...fr...frightened,' Bob's voice shook. 'I...I'll...I'll protect you Dorothy. Oh, look!' He pointed towards the clearing. A large, muscular, twenty-year-old boy appeared. He wore a white vest, his neck covered in gold chains. In his hand, a large hatchet. Dorothy moved close to Baglady.

The boy bounded towards them. They moved back.

'Fecking hell...it's a white Mister T,' Baglady muttered.

The savage leapt onto a tree stump. He yelled out again like a mad polar bear who dropped his last polo mint into the snow. Bob ran but tripped over a branch. He lay on the ground, trembling. Dorothy and

Terry hide behind a tree. Baglady ducked down behind her shopping trolley.

Flexing his muscles, the boy ambled towards them. 'Arrgggghhhhh...put 'em up! Put 'em up.' The boy posed like a boxer waiting for his photo to be taken. 'Which one of you wants it first? Come on. I'll fight you all together if you want! I'll fight you with one hand tied behind my back. I'll fight you standing on one foot.' He balanced on one leg, but nearly toppled backwards. 'I'll fight you with my eyes closed.' He pretended to close his eyes to prove a point.

Baglady picked out an old rusty kettle from her trolley. She held it in her fist.

'Oh, pulling a kettle on me, eh? You, wrinkly old tea-bag, you.' The boy growled.

On hands and knees, Bob couldn't help giggling about the tea-bag comment. 'That's hilarious,' he said, trying to sneak passed the aggressor.

'Oh...sneaking up on me, eh? Hippy boy...I'll chop you with this.' He smashed the hatchet into a tree above the hippy's head. He struggled to get the weapon out of the bark.

Baglady spotted her opportunity. 'Oh you,' the boy turned around just as the hobo's knee connected sweetly with his meat and two veg. He collapsed to the floor like a bag of coal falling off the back of a coal lorry. 'Now fuck off and leave us alone!'

The boy rolled around in agony. In a high-pitched voice, he murmured, 'Jesus, Mary and Judy Garland...what did you do that for? I didn't hurt you.'

'Cos you're a bully;' Baglady stood over him, 'picking on druggy idiots like him.' She pointed to Bob who was only just getting to his feet. A tree branch lodged in his pony-tail.

'Well, you didn't have to hit me.' He looked over at Dorothy. 'Are my balls bleeding?'

'I'll whack you again if you don't stop moaning.'

Dorothy held out her hand to the boy. 'My goodness, what a fuss you're making. Why, you're nothing but a great, big coward!' She helped him up on to his feet.

The boy sat gingerly back down on a tree stump. 'You're right. I am a coward. I even scare myself.'

'Boooo!' hissed Baglady.

The boy curled up in a ball. 'See...I'm a big coward.' Hands covering his face.

Bob poked him in the chest with a twig. 'So why do you act all hard then, when you have obviously...obviously...gone all g...ga...gar...gar...Gareth Thomas on us?'

'Cos' of my family see.'

'Bollocks,' Baglady didn't mince her words.

'It's true,' the boy replied, 'all my family are really, really hard. My gran bit a Copper's ear off in Castle bingo last week.'

Bob's face dropped. 'You're not one of the Murphy's from Swansea Road, are you? The Mad...Mad Murphy's,' he had to peel the words from the inside of his mouth.

The boy nodded his head.

'Who are the Mad Murphy's?' asked Dorothy.

Bob puffed out his cheeks. 'They're full-on, mental heads. They are Merthyr's answer to the Kray Twins mixed with the evilness of the SS.'

Baglady put her arm around the boy. 'Don't mention to your old man or your gran that I booted you in the nuts...will you...I'm sorry...sorry.'

'I won't...promise.'

'What's your name?' Dorothy sat next to him.

'It's...its Rocky,' he almost whispered his reply.

'What?'

'Rocky...It's Rocky.'

'Rocky?' Dorothy responded.

91

He nodded. Bob and Baglady tried to stop themselves from laughing out loud.

'Yeah...It's Rocky, one punch, George Foreman grill, Murphy,' he left a dramatic pause, 'the fifth.'

'The Anti-Rocky, more like!' Bob piped up.

'I know...I'm a sham.'

'So why do you act all tough then?' Baglady butted in.

'Cos' you can't be a Murphy unless you can fight.' Tears filled his eyes, 'and I hate fighting...I hate living this lie. I really wanna be an actor.'

'What?' Bob couldn't resist, 'like Rock-y...Hudson?'

Baglady laughed so hard, she doubled over in pain.

'No,' Rocky stood up, 'no, I wanna tread the real boards...the West End...Broadway.

'Well do it,' said Dorothy.

'Me,' Rocky made a theatrical pose. The back of his right hand touched his forehead, 'on Broadway. My old man wants me to go to Broadmoor.'

'Just talk to him,' said Dorothy.

'He'd kill me.'

'He won't.'

'He fuckin' would,' Baglady interrupted, 'he once broke the milkman's leg for leaving a pint of semi-skimmed milk on our doorstep instead of full-fat.'

'She's right,' Rocky retorted, 'he would...you don't know him. But even if I did...there's nowhere in this town to perform since the Wicked Bitch stopped all funding for arts and development projects.'

Rolling a joint on the stump, Bob looked up. 'Hey, maybe that Wizard dude could help this fluffy, little Tonka toy, too?'

Baglady stamped her feet into the dirt. 'We ain't taking him and all...this is like a primary school trip to Bristol fucking zoo.'

'It will be ok.' Dorothy turned back to the boy, 'do you want to come with us?'

Rocky's eyes lit up, but the smile on his face soon faded. 'But, wouldn't you feel degraded to be seen in my company? I know I would.'

Baglady nodded her head. 'Yeah, we fuckin' would,' she muttered under her breath.

'No, of course not,' beamed Dorothy. 'Shut up, Baglday.'

'Gee, that's...that's awfully nice of you.' Rocky dropped down onto one knee. 'My life thus far has been simply unbearable.'

'Ok let's go,' Dorothy took his arm. 'Come on...sing with me...Oh, we're off to see the Wizard, The Wonderful Wizard of Gurn...OZ.' Rocky joined in. He sung with all his might.

'Oh, fucking hell, look what you have done now, Bob,' Baglady whinged, dragging herself behind them, 'we've got the fucking Proclaimers with us now.'

'My pleasure, me lady.' Bob did a little courtesy.

'Fuck off, junkie!'

From behind a bush, a man dressed in a schoolgirl leotard leapt out. 'I've been a naughty girl. I must be punished.'

Without breaking stride, Baglady booted him full-force in the grape-sacks. He dropped like a stone. 'Now, Ernie Jones from 17 Marshall Crescent...if I was you, I'd fuck off home, or a little birdie will be telling your wife.'

'Oooooooooooohhhhhhhhhhhhhhh, kick me again...go on...that was...lovely...lovely...lovely,' he moaned in pleasure.

Chapter 9
BEAVER

The town hall was rammed packed full of the usual bunch of moaners, groaners, workers and shirkers. Well, truth be known, there were only a handful of actual workers in the room and four of them had been on the sick with 'bard' backs for over three years. However, people had turned up in great numbers to voice their annoyance over the many changes and cuts the council had introduced since the Wicked Bitch had got into power. Lines and lines of angry faces sat impatiently on hard wooden chairs, their eyes fixed on the stage. Most of them had come there looking for a fight, or at least, to land a couple of shy verbal punches!

'Em councillors are the biggest bunch of wankers ever,' a mother of four, breast feeding her new born, loudly informed an elderly gentleman sitting next to her in a shirt and tie. 'Do you know they have made my wheelie bin so small that even Kelly Jones from that band from Snakesville couldn't even fit into it...even if you cut his quiff off?'

'Wheelie quiffs,' the man shrieked, 'never mind fucking wheelie quiffs...this morning I waited three hours to catch a bus to town...three hours....and when one finally showed up...it drove straight passed me...and...and,' his face bright red, 'the driver stuck his V's up and the bus conductor flashed his arse...the cheeky twats. What's public transport coming to these days?'

'If you think that's bad,' a woman in a fake beaver fur hat chipped in, 'yesterday afternoon, I got tasered by a traffic warden in the car park behind the Law Courts.'

'Did they have you for not paying for a ticket or did you overrun the allocated time?' someone asked, 'that's what happened to me!'

'Hang on, this is the best bit, the woman bawled, 'I haven't even got a fucking car. I was only walking through the car park to go to Furniture Zone to buy a bunk bed...the bastards.'

'It's like Nazi Germany around here.'

'Nazis...em traffic wardens are much worse than Nazis...they're like the bouncers from the old Brandy Bridge. 'Em were right evil bastards...all roided up from the Rhondda and all called Dai.'

'Great night club though,' someone piped up.

'Yeah, remember that one night in the summer of '97 and 'em 3 murders...three men stone-cold dead, all before the DJ finished the night off with the smoochie songs. What a great place!'

The tension in the hall grew thicker than the gravy served up on the Castle Hotel's infamous Sunday dinners. A ravenous man with a sharp machete would have struggled to cut it. But things were about to get...even thicker!

To be fair to the councillor in charge of Transportation, walking out onto the stage was one hell of a brave thing to do. Even the Pope would have struggled to get order. In fact, even the Pope, holding a cute puppy, offering free cash and food vouchers, would have been crucified. The poor councillor didn't stand a chance.

'Quiet down please,' the councillor's voice shook as he addressed the audience, 'the Wicked Bitch won't be much longer, she's...she's...she's on an important phone call.' He was economical with the truth, and the audience could sense it.

The first missile missed its intended target. The councillor looked shocked as the free-range egg splattered on the brick wall just behind him. By the time he'd turned back around to voice his displeasure, he got covered from head to toe by the rest of the dozen or so eggs plus a pint of gone-off full fat milk. A loud cheer rose up as the human omelette rushed back off into the wings.

'Go on run, knob head,' an old woman yelled, 'you are faster than the bloody bus service.'

'Why...are we waitin'...why...are we waitin? the crowd belted out a chorus.

The Wicked Bitch could hear the hollering and the singing from the hall but she chose to ignore it. Her office stood eerily quiet. Even the clock on the wall had stopped ticking. Dressed in her familiar black cat suit and thigh high leather boots, she prowled in front of the full-length mirror. A single spotlight lit up her features. Her gimp sat hunched in the corner eating dry corn flakes from a dog bowl.

She was already 45 minutes late. She didn't care. 'Let the fuckers wait,' she hissed at the gimp. He didn't reply. He wasn't allowed. Those were the rules.

She knew the restless masses couldn't do anything about it. Too scared, too predictable. Like rabbits in a cooking pot. 'Let's make them wait a little longer,' she smirked, knowing full well, that most of them would be touching cloth as soon as she strolled out into the room.

She took a last look at the speech, gripped firmly in her hand. A speech she'd been waiting all her life to deliver. In her mind, she was not just the head of the council about to face 526 angry residents, she was Freddie Mercury ready to wow 80,000 fans at Wembley; she was Martin Luther King giving his 'I have a dream' address to a nation; she was Dirty Den telling Angie he didn't love her anymore in the Eastender Christmas Special from 1953 or whatever it was.

She swallowed two, small, green pills while finishing off a can of red bull in one gulp. She glanced across the room. The gimp sat on the floor curled up in a ball around his dog bowl, snoring lightly. The empty container bounced off its head.

'Oh, rubber-tits...get ready...it's show time,' she took a deep breath, 'and don't forget...do exactly what we practised.'

The gimp rushed to the door on all fours. He pressed a button. Out in the hall, the lights dimmed to almost blackness. There was a sharp intake of breath from the waiting audience.

The room fell silent.

'Arrrgghhhh...someone's pinched my handbag,' a woman screamed. 'No....no...its ok...here it is, it fell under my chair.' She bent down to retrieve it. 'Arrggghhhh...someone's pinched my coat now,' she screamed again. On this occasion, she wasn't wrong. Her coat had gone.

Her husband stood up. 'Right,' he raised his voice, 'some thief has pinched my wife's coat and no one is leaving until we find the robbing bastard who's stolen her jacket.'

'That's funny,' a nun burst out laughing, 'who's coat is that jacket?'

'Whose thief is that robber?' someone else piped up.

The husband raced across the room and punched the nun square on the nose. She fell over a row of empty chairs.

Two other nuns leapt like ninjas onto the man's back. A huge fight broke out. Strangely enough, most people decided to punch the one guy in the hall who had a proper job.

'You fuckin' show off,' a man on a mobility scooter drove into the man's back as he curled up in a ball on the floor.

Above the hullabaloo, the theme tune to the Omen blasted out of the speakers positioned in the four corners of the room. The fighting stopped. People sat back down. People gulped, people looked around. Two women fainted. One man in a donkey jacket shat himself. His face bright red as he waddled out of the hall like a penguin with gigantic piles wearing very tight underpants.

Half way through the tune, the Wicked Bitch stepped menacingly out into the centre of the stage. The noise of her footsteps blended in perfectly with the scary music. Flanked by her side, four of the biggest, scariest and dullest bouncers that God had ever put breath into. As a matter of fact, if Heineken made bouncers, they would have looked and acted just like these fuckers.

'Fuck me,' hissed a man quietly, ''em bouncers make the one's all called Dai from the old Brandy Bridge look like the Teletubbies.'

A green spotlight lit the Wicked Bitch's features up.

'Piss my boots, she looks like the Hulk,' a young boy giggled to his mates.

The music drifted away. No one uttered a word. A pin could be heard dropping. One of the bouncers bounded off the stage and threw the old grandmother, who accidently dropped her needle while knitting some baby booties, out through the wooden doors, onto her head.

'And stay out!' All eyes followed the bouncer as he hopped back up onto the stage. A smirk of pleasure fixed on his chiselled puss.

All eyes turned back to the green face of the woman.

'Who the hell are you lot looking at?' the Wicked Bitch snarled at no one in particular. Almost everyone in the audience to a man, or woman, looked at the floor. 'Don't you dare sit there judging me?' She pointed at a man in the front row. Her eyes fixed on his. She didn't speak, just stood motionless, staring. 'Who do you think you are?''

'I'mmmm...I'mmmm...Ernie...Ernie Jones,' said Ernie Jones.

'Ernie Jones, is it?' He nodded. 'So, you are one of the useless twats who can't even get their recycling put in the right boxes.'

'What?'

'Recycling...I've been informed that you, my man, don't know your plastics from your glass bottles. People like you are as much use as a chocolate fireplace.'

'But...but I do my recycling every week...I...I...'

She ignored his pleas of innocence. She turned her back on him and sauntered across the other side of the stage. The bouncers stood arms folded, eyeballing the crowd.

'I used to be like you.' The Wicked Bitch grinned at a woman sitting with her legs crossed near the emergency exit. The woman wearing a tight fitted skirt and low-cut blouse, smiled back at her. 'I did...honest. I used to be poor...shop at Primani.' She sniffed the air. 'Wear cheap perfume just like you.' The woman picked up her handbag and stormed out. The Wicked Bitch knew she was on a roll. She craved the power she commanded.

She stopped opposite a teenager wearing a Weekend Offender tee-shirt. 'I used to be rather pathetic looking, like something off the Jeremy Kyle show. Hey you, boy, did you find out who your real daddy was?' she giggled.

Even though the teenager knew exactly who his father was, in fact his father was sitting next to him, the boy shook his head and muttered, 'No, I didn't. I don't know. Who is he?' He even sounded sorrowful.

His father punched him in the arm. 'Wait until I tell your mother.'

That was the effect the Wicked Bitch had on people. She made them nervous, uncomfortable. People said things they didn't want to say and did things they didn't want to do when she was around. She often popped behind people like some overbearing, intimidating police car suddenly materialising in the rear-view mirror of someone's car. And even though, the driver of that car is innocent of any crime, automatically, they think they have done something wrong and act all nervous. The Wicked Bitch thrived on it. It turned her switch firmly to ON.

'But look at me now. Beautiful, sophisticated.' The Bitch stamped her left foot on the wooden flooring. From the back of the stage, the lid of the silver box in the corner slowly creaked open. The gimp, covered from head to toe in black rubber, rose like a clown in a jack-in-a box. He stood there perfectly still.

Mouths dropped to the floor. Even the bouncers took a sly peek.

'Fuck me, its Frank Bough,' someone near the emergency exit whispered quietly.

The Wicked Bitch didn't break stride. 'I wear the best clothes, eat at the finest restaurants. Of course, not in Merthyr, I don't want to get food poisoning. I go to proper places...Cardiff...Swansea...even Aberdare.' She waited for the moans and the groans to die down. 'Because, they serve the best snake and chips in the world over here,' she cracked a joke.

The nun laughed. 'Snake and chips...now, that is funny.'

The Holy woman's feet didn't touch the ground. Two bouncers threw her out into the street. She landed on her head, or to be more precise, she landed on her habit next to the 'pin-dropping' old woman.

'Not as funny as flying fucking penguins,' the Wicked Bitch snorted to the crowd. No one dared smirk, never mind think of laughing out loud. She stamped her feet for the second time. Her gimp crawled over on all fours, tongue protruding like an anteater at an all-you-can-eat red and black ant buffet. She clipped a dog lead onto his neck. She walked around the stage, dragging her rubber-clad slave behind her. People were too shocked to speak. Even Doris Morgan, who had won competitions for talking non-stop, fell silent.

'Now I'm the most feared and most respected person in this entire town,' the Bitch continued, 'no...probably the country. War heroes, boxers and do-gooders don't deserve statues littering up my streets. There should be a statue of me...for everything I have done for this god-forsaken town.'

She posed, one hand pointed to the sky, as if chiselled out of the finest Italian marble. The gimp copied her. Some of the audience nodded their heads in agreement, or more like, nodded their heads in case she spied them not nodding their heads.

'How did I get to where I am today, I hear you ask?'

Silence. She repeated her questions. Still silence. From the back, the thug boy in the Burberry hat and his sidekick stood up. In perfect harmony, they yelled out, 'How did you get to where you are today, then love?'

One bouncer went to jump off the platform. The Wicked Bitch stopped him. 'No...it's ok. Thank you, boys.' The smile on Thug boy's face looked similar to the smirk on a cat's face who had licked up all of the clotted cream. 'Let me tell you, it wasn't easy. I worked hard and slaved away doing endless jobs for no thanks and piteous of a pay, then I saw the light, or the darkness and I sold my soul to the devil...I got a job working for Merthyr council...which is 10 times better than working for R.C.T in the Rhondda, let me tell you.'

The crowd didn't know if they should cheer or boo. They did both at the same time, which sounded odd. The gimp positioned on his knees, made a wanking movement with his right hand every time the word 'council' got mentioned.

'I didn't like it at first...working for the council.' Another long wanking stroke from the gimp. People sat biting their lips, trying not to laugh. 'Boring...nothing to do but go to lunch, drink coffee and fiddle my expenses.' The gimp noticed people watching him. He played up to the crowd. He bent down and started to lick his master's boots. 'However, one day,' she added, 'I sat looking about the office in the town hall. Everyone was asleep as usual but then it struck me, I was better than all of that lot. They were nothing more than fresh dog shit on my stilettoes.'

The gimp stopped what he was doing. He started to pretend to heave and wipe his tongue with his rubber covered hands. Everyone started giggling, even the bouncers. The gimp loved the sudden attention. At last, he was a shining star, not the darkness.

Unaware of the rubber-clad comedian by her side, the Bitch continued, 'I thought, why I couldn't run this town? It goes without saying...there were a couple of things I had to take care of...a few old things standing in my way.' Lost in some violent sadistic world of her own, she began twisting the lead around the gimp's neck several times. He began to choke. Without warning, she marched off to the other side of the stage, dragging the poor gimp with her. The gimp wriggled on the ground. Under his rubber mask his face changed from white, to red, to blue. People worried for his safety. After a full two minutes of twisting and rolling and struggling about on the floor, he began tickling his nipples and rubbing his groin. He let out a soft moan. His erection obvious to everyone looking on.

'He likes it,' at the back of the room, Thug boy hissed, 'he bloody well likes it.'

'I bet it's Michael Hutchins in disguise,' whispered Sidekick.

'Who's he?'

'He's that dead singer from that pop band from New Zealand.'

A man in a tweed jacket in front of them, turned around and said, 'It was Australia actually.'

'Fuck off Mister Hill...just cos you're a Geometry teacher. We ain't in school now.'

'It is a Geography teacher actually, Jenkins.'

'Same horse, different fuckin' jockey,' Thug boy grunted, 'so keep your beak out.'

Sidekick nudged Thug Boy's arm. 'Look...it is him...It is the INXS singer...I bet he's going to pull an orange out of his pocket.'

'He hasn't got pockets in that gimp suit?'

'He has...look I can see an orange shape.'

'That's not an orange, that's probably his erection.'

Thug Boy raised his hissing up a little bit, 'What? You're telling me that, that gimps got a cock the shape of a fucking orange?'

'Yep.'

'What's his nickname then? Cock-Gimp Orange?'

'Very funny, but no,' said Sidekick, 'It's Tangerine Todger.'

The woman in the fake beaver fur hat chipped in. 'How about Satsuma Sack?'

A few people near them laughed.

'More like Blood Orange Bollocks,' Thug Boy sniggered.

The Geography teacher turned back around. 'Will you be quiet please...I'm trying to listen to what the woman is saying.'

The Geography teacher didn't see the two, huge bouncers racing through the crowd towards them all. Thug boy and Sidekick did. They slumped back down in their seats, mouth firmly shut.

'At last,' were the last two words the Geography teacher muttered that night. In point of fact, they were the last two words the teacher muttered for several months. Having his jaw broken in three places behind the skip by the back door put pay to that.

The Wicked Bitch didn't bat an eyelash as the bouncer's dragged the poor teacher out towards the back doors by his ankles. She grinned and carried on, 'but then a few of the older, more established councillors suddenly upped and died...mysteriously...tragically...and thankfully very painfully.' The gimp pretended to stab out with a dagger, psycho-style. 'They deserved it...nothing but a bunch of money-grabbin' bastards...do you agree Merthyr?' Some people nodded. 'Yes, I thought so...come on everyone repeat after me...All the councillors except for the Wicked Bitch are a bunch of old money-grabbin' bastards.'

The chorus started out quite quiet but by the end everyone in the room stood yelling out at the top of their voices, 'All the councillors except for the Wicked Bitch are a bunch of old money-grabbin' bastards.'

The Bitch smirked, under her blouse her nipples stood hard and erect; she even got a little damp down below. The gimp, who had joined in, got lost in the moment. His muffled voice carried on long after everyone else had stopped. The Bitch turned sharply and kicked him in the ribs. He slumped. 'I didn't tell you, idiot.' She turned back to audience. 'Within no time I climbed the ladder. It was my destiny...my calling...And now...I stand before you...the cherry on the top of the cake...the boss...the number one, numero uno, top cat...your ruler...your better half...probably one day, your queen.' The gimp clambered back on all fours. He positioned himself into a seat, or better still, her human throne. The Wicked Bitch sat down on his back. She even did a few little queen waves to each corner of the room. In her mind, she rode a horse drawn carriage through the packed mean streets of her town. Ticker tape rained down from the council flats; people waved and cheered as she went past. Girls threw rose petals onto the road in front of her.

One bloke in the crowd (probably a plant) held up a plaque announcing his love for the beautiful, council leader.

The perfect image got rudely ripped from the grasp of her mind, when from the back, the Thug Boy and Sidekick jumped up and sang, 'I see a little silhouette of a man Scaramouch, scaramouch will you do the Fandango.'

Everyone turned. One or two of the dull ones in the audience joined in until the Bitch screamed out. 'No...not like Freddie bloody Mercury, you fucking idiots. Where are you from?' she pointed at Thug boy.

With pride written all over his face, the Thug boy replied, '12A Cherry Grove, it's in the Gurnoz, love...it's the one with the fridge in the garden.'

'Do you want to be my gimp?' the Wicked Bitch pointed at the boy. He glanced at the man in rubber, feverishly nodding his head.

'No ta, love.'

'Then, be quiet or I will get someone to fuck you back off to 12A Cherry Grove and shove you in that fuckin' fridge in the garden. Understand?'

At first, both teenagers refused to budge. They both stood defiant, arms folded, baseball caps tilted to the side on their greasy heads. The biggest bouncer growled at them. They both sat down.

On the stage, the speech continued. 'I have a dream you know,' the Wicked Bitch raised her voice, 'I have a dream that one day from the ludicrous number of speed-bumps up on the council estates, to the gang-land battles in the comprehensive schoolyards, From the two-headed babies born in Prince Charles hospitals, to the swinger's houses in the posh part of town.' The gimp did the actions. 'You will all thank me for what I have done for this town. I have put us on the map. You will all sing my name and wear tee-shirts with my image embossed onto it. And maybe mugs, tea towels...underwear...bingo pens. And when I close that drug rehabilitation centre up on the Gurnoz and get rid of the wizard...this town will be mine...all mine.' She let go of the evilest laugh that had ever been recorded in evilest laugh history.

People clapped, actually clapped!

'So, stop all this moaning and complaining. I'm making all these changes for your own good...the good of the town. To make us the best goddamn town in Wales...The UK...the World.' She stared off into the distance.

The bloke in the tie went to say something but the bouncer pointed at him.

'So, if that is all,' she cried, 'I suggest you get back to work or whatever else you do...and stop wasting my bloody time.' She started to walk off.

The gimp stood his ground, pretended to laugh, holding his sides.

The Bitch stormed back. 'Get back in the fucking box, you idiot.'

She thundered off. Under his mask, the gimp looked sad. He crawled to the box, picked an orange from his pocket and put it in his mouth. He closed the lid. The lights went off in the entire building.

'I told you, I was right,' said Sidekick, 'that gimp bloke thing is Michael Hutchins.'

Chapter 10

MONKEYS

Hand in hand, Dorothy, Bob, Baglady, and Rocky hiked through the long grass of the cop fields located on the outskirts of Galon Uchaf. Behind them, Terry the dog sniffed about in the undergrowth. The mutt was feeling rather randy and needed to empty "the pipes" as they say.

The Cop Fields weren't so much a lush green oasis, more like a tump of wasteland covered in weeds, noisy frogs having sex and stingee nettles.

'The bloody Cop-fields...I lived here once for four months,' Baglady muttered, 'over there in that large sewerage pipe.' She pointed at a large grey concrete pipe covered in spray-can penises located in the far corner of the field.

'Why do they call it the Cop-Fields?' asked Dorothy.

Rocky put his hand up, 'It's where all the schoolboys bring their girlfriends to cop-a-feel...I heard...get it...cop-a field.'

'Bollocks,' Bob piped up, 'it's called that 'cos Copper was mined here back in the days.'

'Copper! What? Real Copper?' asked Dorothy.

'No, plastic Copper. Of course, real Copper!'

'Hang on,' Baglady interrupted them, 'you're all wrong. If you must know, it's called the Cop-fields because during the Great Galon

Uchaf Drug Wars of '73, two undercover drug enforcement Coppers got captured, tortured, tarred and feathered and finally murdered.'

'Murdered!' the rest yelled.

'Yeah...and they are buried over there...where your dirty mutt is taking a shit.'

(Who knows...maybe that will be a new book?)

'Is that true?' asked Dorothy. Baglady nodded her head.

'So, is Postman Pat Park up in Pant named that for the same reason, but only with murdered postmen called Pat?' asked Rocky.

'Probably,' replied Baglady, 'these postmen are a bunch of c**ts...what is it about them wearing fucking shorts all the time? In the fucking winter, as well. Fucking show-offs. I'd have killed them myself if I had a gun.'

'Never mind who murdered who,' Bob placed his hands on his hips and puffed out his cheeks. 'I'm starving mun...I've got the munchies right on me.'

'Well stop smoking that stuff then,' Baglady grunted, 'and you won't have the munchies right on you.'

'It's not that stuff...it's the...it's the...what was the question again?' He looked about in a daze.

Dorothy stood on an old tyre. 'How much further have we got to go?'

'It can't be that far now,' Rocky replied, 'Listen.' Overhead the sound of mechanical whirling filled the skies.

'Is that a dragonfly?'

'A dragonfly?' Rocky almost yelled, 'of course it's not a dragonfly...it's a helicopter.'

'Oh,' said Dorothy, looking up, 'I've never seen a helicopter before.'

'Hang on a minute,' said Bob, 'how bloody big are dragonflies where you live?'

'About this big,' she held her fingers about 12 inches apart.

'Bloody hell bells...that's not a dragonfly, that's a Pterodactyl.'

The helicopter came into sight over the top of the prefabs.

'What is it doing?' Dorothy asked again.

'I'll tell her, let me tell her,' Rocky jumped about, waving his hand in the air. 'Chasing joy riders. They're chasing joyriders.'

'Joy riders?'

'Yeah...you know, teenagers who pinch cars and drive around until they get chased by police helicopters?'

'Why?'

'Beats working in McDonalds or burning down schools, I guess.'

'No, but why chase them in a helicopter, wouldn't it be better to chase them in a car?'

Joint balancing from his bottom lip, Bob chipped in, 'of course it would...but them pigs like to show off their new toys.' He looked up to the grey sky, 'I've seen a dragon fly, I've seen a horse-fly, but I've never seen a pig flyyyyyy.' He flicked his V's up at the helicopter. 'Fuuuuuccckkkkk Offffff Pigs.'

Baglady snapped them all back to reality. 'Can we keep moving...it's not far? Just over this field and through the estate.'

Dorothy sat down on the grass, fiddling with her shoes. 'But can we have a rest my feet are killing me?'

'Well take those bloody stupid shoes off then,' snapped Baglady, 'you look like you are going for a boogie upstairs in the fucking Three Horse Shoes.'

'I'm cream krackered as well,' Bob laid down next to her, 'and I need some nosh. I would kill Bob Dylan for a Hobnob at this moment.' He made the sign of the cross and looked up to the sky, 'sorry Bob but I've got the hunger games right on me.'

'Oooooohhhh yeah' Dorothy licked her lips, 'I'm hungry as well.'

'Are you hungry Terry? Bob picked the dog up. 'Sausagesssss,' Bob barked like a dog.

Rocky stood in front of them all. 'And I'm wasting away here. Dorothy, does my bum look thin in this?' He stuck his rear close to her face.

Baglady tutted loudly. 'Wasting away...wasting a-way...a bloody camel would keel over before you lot.' They all looked at her. 'OK...ok...I'll knock something up, but then we're off. Deal?'

Silence.

'Deal, I said?'

'Deal,' they all muttered back.

Baglady rummaged about in her shopping trolley. She pulled out a large fish bone, a three-day old half eaten bag of cold chips and some other unsavoury items which she thought would be better not to show her dinner guests. 'Fit for a bloody king...give me ten minutes.' She disappeared behind a large tree.

The other three sat down on the grass. Seeing the tight rear of a rabbit a few metres away, Terry licked his lips before chasing after the furry, sexy creature.

'I need another spliff to get me in the mood for some grub.' Bob rolled an extra-large joint. 'God...she's a weird one, isn't she?' He lit the end. The smoke sailed up into the air.

'Who?' Dorothy took her shoes off. Her toes matted in dirt.

'Good god, Dorothy, your feet are bumping,' Rocky held his nose.

'Her,' Bob pointed to where the Baglady had disappeared to, 'Chewbacca...the human toilet brush.' His Chewbacca style cry made them all laugh.

'How old do you think she is?' Dorothy asked.

'130...at least.' Bob took another tote.

'That's old, isn't it?'

'She smells like she's dead,' Rocky piped up, 'she smells worse than your feet, Dorothy.'

The Baglady's voice pierced the afternoon air. 'I can bloody hear you, you know.' They all jumped. 'I'll 130 you lot. Now, Hippy boy, make sure they don't get into trouble...or else.'

'What?'

'You fucking heard me...Ice fucking Tea-bag...now stay out of trouble...the food won't be long.'

Bob made a stern face. 'She swears more than Gordon fucking Ramsey but she's got more facial hair.' Dorothy giggled. Bob finished the spliff with a one almighty long puff. He fell back on the grass, his head full of smoke and weird thoughts.

Behind the mountain of empty KFC boxes discarded by thoughtless youths in stolen cars, Terry pinned the poor rabbit to the floor. He gave it a dirty old grin before going in, bare backed. The rabbit yelped.

'I'm so hungry,' Dorothy reached out into the grass. 'Hey what are these things?' Picking up a mushroom she showed it to Bob.

'Those my dear...are mushrooms maaaaaannnn...magic ones.'

'Magic? Why are they magic?'

The dope had gone straight to Bob's head. He struggled to think, never mind talk. 'Cos...they just maggggiiiiicccccc.'

'Are they ok to eat?'

'Yeah, but you better...you better...not...cos...cos...' mid-sentence, he fell backwards onto the grass. He lay fast asleep, a warm, contented grin on his face.

Dorothy tasted one. 'Oh, not bad, and part of my 5 a day I guess,' she muttered.

Rocky knelt down next to her. He popped one in his mouth. 'That tastes earthy...its tastes exactly like...like...' Dorothy waited, 'hummmmmm...oh...never mind.' Rocky's cheeks glowed bright red.

The pair spent the next five minutes devouring as many mushrooms as they could find. Meanwhile Bob slept like a baby and Terry the dog fucked the unfortunate rabbit like a rampant John Holmes in a dog-skin fur coat in a 70's porno movie.

The magic and the mystery of the mushrooms didn't take long to kick in. In Dorothy's mind, some odd, weird trippie music began to play. 'Where's that music coming from?' She looked around to try to find its source.

Looking rather pleased with himself, Terry staggered back towards them like John Wayne after a 100-mile horse ride across the Texas plains. If he smoked he would have been puffing on a well-earned cigarette as he walked. Dorothy picked him up. She rubbed the dog in Bob's face. 'Wake up...Bob...Bob...wake up.'

Bob let out a scream. 'Jesus Christ, I thought it was the thing licking my chops.'

Rocky burst out laughing. 'The thing...what Baglady? That's funny.'

Out of the blue, Dorothy marched about, screeching out random things in a thick Scottish accent. 'Yeah, she does look a bit like the thing.'

Rocky felled on his back, feet up in the air, laughing like a dying fly.

Bob looked at them both in turn. 'How many of those mushrooms have you had?'

'Only about 40!' Dorothy sounded like one of the Krankies trying to do an impression of Sean Connery. She marched about, thinking she was playing the bagpipes.

'40!' yelled Bob.

'Don't lie,' Rocky rolled about in the grass, 'you had 200, the same as me.'

'Fuckin' hell!' Bob immediately sobered up from the effects of the weed, 'she'll kill me.'

'I will walk five hundred miles...and I will walk five hundred mooooorrrrreeeeeeee.' Dorothy and Rocky bounded about, arm in ram.

'Oh, fuck no, they have turned into the fuckin' Proclaimers...she will definitely kill me now.'

The two mushroom virgins were both experiencing the happy side of the hallucinatory drug. That soon changed. Overhead the sky went dark. The helicopter circled around again. This time Dorothy really thought it was a dragonfly. A dragonfly with the face of the clown from the movie IT.

'Arrggghhhhhhh,' she screeched. 'Get away...get away from me.' She hid behind a tree, swiping at the giant flying machine as if she was swatting flies. She twitched. First her right eye, then her arms. Then one leg.

To the postman, taking a short cut through the field, she looked like she was either having a fit or dancing to the birdy song. He carried on regardless. He was more concerned with the fact his shorts were a little too tight and rubbing the inside of his postman's thighs.

'The monsters are coming...the monsters are coming,' Rocky yelled, rolling around on his belly.

'Oh...Oh...what's happening?' Dorothy put her head in her hands. 'I feel odd. Terry, Terry...what's wrong with Terry?' In her mind, her dog had transformed into an evil beast with the face of Debbie McGee. She didn't know which was worse, the McGee dog or the dragonfly clown.

Bob raced between each of them, trying to calm them down. 'Look...sit down...be quiet...please.'

'MONKEYS...MONKEYS,' Rocky bellowed.

'What do you mean Monkeys?'

Rocky swatted invisible things off his chest. 'Monkeys, monkeys, monkeys...everywhere.'

Bob grabbed Rocky by the arms. 'Monkeys...like the ones off the PG tips advert?' Rocky shook his head. 'What? Monkeys like the pop group the monkeys? Hey, hey we're the monkeys.' Rocky shook his head again and flapped his arms like a giant eagle at a rave. 'Don't tell me...flying monkeys...you don't want to see flying monkeys when you're trippin.'

Rocky's eyes bugled out of his head, 'NO...worse.'

Bob put both hands on his hips. 'What could possibly be worse than flying monkeys?'

'Shagging monkeys...look.' he pointed towards the tree where in his imagination he could clearly see a fictitious shagging monkey standing on the branches with a big strap-on invisible banana attached to his groin.

'Where?' Bob looked about.

'There...in the tree...can't you see it?'

'No...it's ok...there's nothing there...it's in your imagination....it's only the drugs.'

'Arrrggghhhhhhhhh, I can see it as well,' Dorothy screamed.

'No, you can't,' shrieked Bob.

'I can...I can. There he is...there...in the tree.'

Terry the dog barked in the direction of where the monkey would be if it was real.

'Not you as well,' said Bob.

'Oh my god, he's coming after us,' Rocky cried, 'RUN!'

The fictitious shagging monkey leapt off the tree in slow motion. His strap-on banana penis throbbed so hard it was like a heating pipe in the engine room of a ship before it was about to explode.

Dorothy ran. Rocky ran. Terry ran. Although Bob couldn't see the monkey, he knew from past experience that it didn't mean the imaginary creature wasn't real. Once after a session on an extremely strong strain of dope from Amsterdam and a flagon of White Lightening cider, he played basketball for three and a half hours with an invisible ten-foot Indian who lived in the basement of the Buffalo's pub in town.

So, Bob ran.

The shagging monkey chased the gang around and around and around the tree. To make the scene even funnier a car driving passed at that exact moment blasted out the theme tune to the Benny Hill show on its super, duper stereo system. *(On my life, you couldn't make it up...well....)*

'Is he still behind us?' Bob asked, afraid to look.

'He sure is,' Rocky replied, 'and his banana is much bigger now.'

Round and round they ran. The grin on the monkey's face getting more sinister with each lap.

The hairy creature upped the pace. It was within touching distance of Rocky. Looking behind him, the frightened boy didn't see the large stone sticking out of the ground. He hit it with his toe, tripped and fell. During the fall, and as if he was the star appearing in some kind of hardcore gay porno movie made in a posh penthouse in the hills of LA, Rocky's trousers split right down the middle. His bare arse exposed to the elements.

The shagging monkey skidded to a halt. It grinned; it twirled its bushy, black eyebrow in its hairy fingers before spraying some mouth freshener into its gob. Rocky couldn't move, too scared to even look behind. Instead he made the sign of the cross at exactly the moment the shagging monkey's horny banana entered his tunnel of love. The shriek stopped Bob and Dorothy in their tracks. They turned to see what was going on.

Dorothy could see the monkey bumming the poor boy quite vividly. Bob still couldn't see it, but years and years of drugs abuse had given him a good imagination. He could picture the distressing scene. Terry the dog got a hard-on and lined up behind the monkey in case there was chance of sloppy seconds floating about.

Baglady appeared, holding four paper plates full of grub. She dropped them in shock. 'What the heck is going on here? Where the hell did that shagging monkey come from? Have you lot been taking drugs?'

Everything stopped still except for the sexual rhythmic movement of the monkey and the soft moans of Rocky, who to be honest by them was starting to enjoy the experience.

Bob shook his head. 'Of course, they haven't been taking drugs.'

Baglady pushed passed him. 'Dorothy, have you been taking drugs?'

The girl looked at her. 'Celtic 5, Rangers 3 and a half.'

'Bob,' Baglady screamed, 'what the hell have you give them?'

'Nothing!'

'BOB!'

'Ok...they may have had a magic mushroom or 2.'

'2?'

'Hundred.'

'Two hundred magic mushrooms...for fuck sake...I only left you all for fifteen minutes. I told you to look after them.' She pointed at the shagging monkey, 'and you, Russel fuckin' Brand, you bum him one more time, you, you hairy freak and you'll be eating that banana out of a blender for a month.' She slapped the creature full force on his balls with a stick.

The monkey doubled up in pain and hobbled away.

'Call me!' Rocky mouthed to the invisible beast.

Dorothy twitched more violently. Rocky crawled around on the ground like a worm. Terry sniffing around him, his little red lipstick sticking out of its hairy container.

Baglady spoke. 'Bob, I could kill you for this.'

'What did I do? Hang on...how did you see the monkey? I couldn't.'

'Never mind that...look at the state of them. Right, I'll help Rob Roy here,' she placed her arm around Dorothy's shoulders, 'you catch Willy the wiggling Worm over there.'

The Baglady gently placed her arm around the scared girl's shoulders. 'Come on Dorothy, love...let's get you to a safe place until these nasty mushrooms wear off.' She growled in Bob's direction again.

'Well, I will wank 500 miles, and I will wank 500 more,' Dorothy sung at the top of her voice.

They headed towards the large concrete sewage pipe covered in spray-can penises.

Chapter 11

BILLY BESSY

'Look at the fuckin' state of 'em lot,' a kid shouted from his position on top of the garages behind the prefabs, 'they look like the fuckin' Krankies.'

Even though, there are only two in the Krankies and there were four people in Dorothy's gang, the rest of the kids, also on the garage roof, laughed as if their spotted faced leader was the ghost of Bob Monkhouse.

'Just ignore them,' Baglady led the way through the little alleyway at the back of the houses towards the Gurnoz.

'Oh Krankies...listen to your grandmother now.'

'Hey,' Baglady turned to face the gang, 'I know your mother, Colin Hunt. She's doing a course in the college with your gran, ain't she?'

The boy shrugged his shoulders. 'I'm not sure.'

'Yeah she is...prostitution in four easy stages...I heard she's the star pupil in the class. She had an A star in anal studies.'

'Fuck off,' the boy yelled, 'my mother is a filler on the dark chocolate line in OP Chocolates.'

'The only thing your mother gets filled is her dark chocolate starfish. Fiver a pop I heard.'

Everyone laughed. Even members of the gang laughed. Well, until the leader of the yobs pushed the fat one off the roof. The boy landed inside an old burnt out skip.

'We better go,' Rocky muttered.

This time the others didn't argue. They carried on walking the opposite way to the garages and the pack of irate boys.

'Can't you cover yourself up?' Baglady snapped at Rocky, as the back of his trousers flapped about in the wind.

'I can't.'

'I'm still hungry,' muttered Bob

'You can fuck off as well Hippy boy...'

'Hang on a minute,' Dorothy stopped in her tracks, 'where's Terry?'

'Who's Terry?' Bob grunted. They all looked at him, 'I'm only fuckin' joking...God has everyone lost their sense of humour?'

'But, where is he?' She shouted his name again.

'Knowing that randy bastard, he's probably up to his nuts in some beaver's vag.' Baglady didn't break stride. 'He needs some bromide in his Pedigree chum.'

'Terry...Terry,' Dorothy frantically bellowed. 'Terry...Terry. We've got to find him.'

Baglady groaned. 'Ok...let's spread out and look for the randy old twat...but I'm warning you all now...if I get back and he,' she pointed at Rocky, 'is getting bummed again by some invisible shagging monkey or getting bummed by anything...I'm fuckin' off.'

Rocky frowned. 'But I can't go walking around with this hole in my trousers...That's just asking for someone to...to abuse me.' Inside him, something stirred.

'Ok, Magic Mike,' Baglady enhanced, 'you stay here in case the mutt turns up.'

'But what about those kids on the garages, they may pick on me.'

'Rocky...they're only about fourteen years old. Man up. Boy.' She turned around, 'Bob, you take First and Second Avenue.'

'Right, Commandant...and when we find him, me will gas him,' he joked.

'Fuck up Bob. Dorothy, you take third and fourth avenue...and I will take sixth and seventh.'

'What about Fifth Avenue?' Dorothy asked.

The others all laughed. They didn't stop chuckling for a full five minutes. 'Dorothy love,' Baglady smirked, 'a few things you must know. No one, not even the police in fucking tanks go through Fifth Avenue. Did you know that last week, a gang of Russian football hooligans tried to walk down there? Twenty-odd of the tough Ruskie fuckers, all marching down there in black tee-shirts, gumshields and muscles...they haven't been seen since!!!'

'Oh no...but what if Terry's gone down there?'

Bob made a knife across his throat sign. 'If he has, he's swimming next to the fishes now.'

'What does that mean?'

'It means by now he's probably been killed, skinned, cooked and is the filling in a juicy beef and ale pie in the Fish shop'

'Oh no...don't say that...quick let's go.' Dorothy took off her shoes.

While they all spilt off in different directions, Rocky hid in an old telephone box. Shaking like a leaf, he watched streams of men, paper under their arms, marching into the Betting Office opposite. No one ever came back out. It was like a gambling Tardis for the desperate and unemployed.

BOOSH!

A sandy brick bounced off the glass of the box. Rocky screamed out. The gang of school kids surrounded him like Indians surrounding a posse of wagon trains but on a much smaller scale. Although one of the kids was holding a machete and had the fur of a dead cat tucked into his snake-belt.

'Go away,' Rocky muttered.

The gang of savages tried to wrestle open the door. Rocky held the handle of the door tight. His fingers white. One kid poked a stick through a broken pane. The sharp point pierced Rocky's bare arse.

'Oooohhh, get off. Go away,' he tried to sound manly but failed.

The door shot open. Rocky cowered in the corner. The ruffians dragged him, kicking and screaming, out of the vandalized telephone box by his ankles.

'What shall we do with him?' one boy, whose balls hadn't yet dropped, shrieked in a high-pitched voice.

'Beat him up?' another yelped.

'Not yet,' said the leader.

'Scalp him,' grunted the boy holding the machete.

'Later,' the leader grinned, 'I know, tie him to the lamppost.'

'Yes,' came the reply.

Rocky resisted but they were like a pack of hungry Hyenas bringing down a helpless wildebeest. He didn't stand a chance. They clung on to him until he had no strength left. Using old rope, they secured him to the nearest lamp post. Apparently, it was the same lamppost their fathers had tied, tarred and feathered Shakin Steven two years before when he sung up the Martyrs Club before he was super famous. Shakey never ever came back to Merthyr.

'What shall we do with him now?' one of the kids asked.

'Let's tickle him?' said one of the newer and more innocent members of the gang.

'Fuck that...let's burn him?' shouted another.

'Yes...let's light him up,' said the leader, 'who's got matches?'

There was a break in the hollering and yelping as they all rummaged about in their pockets looking for matches. With empty hands, they all shrugged their shoulders.

'We haven't got any matches, bloody typical,' the leader hissed, 'What else could we do to him?'

They all stood around the prisoner, thinking out loud and rubbing their chins a lot.

'How about if we cover him in custard and lick it off,' some kid with a bonky eye muttered, pulling a tin of custard out of his satchel. They all turned and stared at the boy. 'What? That's what my grampie makes his dog, Boris, do to him.'

Rocky started screaming.

'Stop screaming.'

Rocky screamed louder.

'Put a sock in his mouth,' the leader commanded.

'Whose sock?' bonky eye boy asked.

'Yours.'

'I'm not taking my socks off. They were clean on, last Thursday.'

'I know...let's cut the rest of his clothes off and paint him bright yellow...like the yellow-bellied Swansea Roader that he is.'

'YESSSSS,' nodded the leader. The rest of the gang agreed.

Someone produced a scissors and they proceeded, with glee, to remove Rocky of all his clothes.

'Right,' the leader clapped his grubby hands, 'who's got the yellow paint?'

They all stood about waiting for someone else to answer the question.

'That was a stupid fuckin thing to say,' the leader poked the offending boy in the chest. 'Paint him yellow you said...with what? Fresh air?'

'We could paint him with my custard.'

'Shut up!'

'But that's yellow.'

'I know...but we ain't painting him with custard...it would look girly.'

'My step-dads got some fence stain in our shed...Cuprinol,' said the newer and more innocent gang member.

123

'Is it yellow?'

'No...I'm sure his fences are Mexican Brown I think.'

'Ok that will do...go and get it...and see if your mothers got any of them Jammy Dodgers left.'

'What are we going to do with them?' said the kid with the bonky eye, 'stick them up his bum? Yeah...yeah...I'll do it.'

'I'm going to eat them, you fucking weirdo.'

Rocky fainted.

Meanwhile, in the cold, damp streets of Galon Uchaf, Dorothy wasn't having any luck either. Everywhere seemed deserted. But then off in the distance, she heard shouting. Some kind of hullabaloo. Around the corner leading into Third Avenue, a large group of people gathered. Some of them held up homemade placards. Some held homemade fire torches made from wood and rags.

'OUT...OUT...OUT,' the crowd chanted at one of the houses.

Dorothy walked amongst them.

Out of the blue, a man raced up to the front fence, anger etched all over his face. He let out a cry as he chucked a rock, the size of a tortoise, straight through the upstairs window of the house. The glass exploded into a million pieces. The crowd cheered.

'What's going on?' Dorothy asked a girl standing on the edge of the crowd.

'You won't believe it,' the girl grunted, 'it's disgusting...I'm in shock. He's worse than a kiddie fiddler or a mass murderer in my eyes...much, much worse.'

'Who is?'

'Him, him in there. Mister Do-gooder. Do you know what he's done?'

Dorothy shrugged. 'Killed someone?'

'Worse?'

'Worse than killing someone...bloody hell...it must be serious.'

'Yeah, it is much worse. He only gone and taxed his fuckin' car?'

'What?'

'Yeah, you heard me correctly. The twat's taxed his car.'

A boy, holding a lit petrol bomb, piped up as he rushed passed, 'I also heard his kids don't even claim for free school dinners.' He despatched the Molotov Cocktail into the garden. It smashed up against the porch. Six-foot flames licked the side of the house.

'Fuckin' hell bells...that's the straw that broke the zebra's spine,' said the girl, 'I'm going to burn his fucking house down. He's made us up on this estate into a laughing stock in Merthyr. I bet you Freddie Emotion from Dowlais Top is already tweeting about it.'

She checked her phone. 'He has...hear this...Galon Uchaf has now officially gone all posh as man taxes car...what next?' smiley face. Hashtag, poshwankers.

'He's a sarcastic cunt that Freddie Emotion...just cos he's never worked in his life. He's spot on though. He should be the fuckin' Mayor.'

BANG!

Someone torched the man's car. It exploded. Part of the front passenger's seat shot through the window-screen and landed on the road, still on fire. Kids and old women danced around it like manic zombie creatures at an open-air zombie music festival, which involved strong class A drugs and zombie house music.

'Have you seen my dog?' Dorothy asked the girl. 'He's about this big.'

'How long it's been missing?' the girl asked.

'Only about an hour.'

The girl made a face. 'Probably already in the fish shop. I love their dog steak and ale pies. But not as good as their special mince and cat pasties...they are fuckin' lush.'

Dorothy let go of a scream before racing off to find the little fish shop of horrors. There she found her pet showing off around some bitch on heat.

'Bark me,' Terry puckered up his dog lips. The bitch gave him a seductive doggy smile.

Luckily for her, and him, the fish shop had closed for the day and the animal catcher employed to supply them with fresh meat was off with a slight head cold.

Dorothy picked up Terry and cwtched him tightly. 'Terry, I've been worried sick.'

Back near the garages, Rocky opened his eyes. 'What the heck?' He found himself being carried, fireman lift style, on a pair of muscular broad shoulders.

'Arrrrrgghhh, whose legs are them?' he cried out when he saw his own bare, brown legs. What he hadn't realised was when he had fainted, the little savages had applied the first coat of varnish to his hairy limbs. From a distance he looked like a Double Decker chocolate bar.

'Put me down,' he demanded, 'put me down.'

'Two minutes and we'll be home,' a gruff voice answered him back.

'Home? Where's home?' Rocky was almost too afraid to ask. He didn't know if he was getting carried out of the frying pan straight into someone's fire.

'Home is where the heart is,' the man said, 'and this is where my heart is.' He carried Rocky in through the front door, through the small hallway and plonked him down on the old-fashioned settee. The man threw him a tea-towel to cover up himself up.

The house smelled of dust and cheap perfume. It reminded Rocky of how his gran's house smelt before she retired from the family drug running business and went to live in Benidorm.

Rocky looked down at his naked brown legs. 'Thank god, they only got my legs,' He checked the rest of his body.

'Thanks to me, Butt' the man spoke to him. 'If I hadn't turned up you would have been the Creosol man by now. To be honest, I was going to wait until they had finished just to see what you would look like. It would have been so bloody funny. But then I thought better of it.'

The old man winked at him. The first thing Rocky noticed about his rescuer was how rugged he looked. His face hard as a lump of coal. His hands like shovels. Not big in height, maybe 5 feet 4, but he was nearly the same size across. He wore a long grey over coat and steel-capped boots.

'Lucky for you I'd just finished my shift in the iron works...crane driver, me...forty-five years, man and boy.'

'Thank you, Mister.'

'Do you want a nice mug of strong tea?'

Rocky nodded, 'Yes, please...but not too strong...quite weak actually...a bit like me.'

The man laughed. 'Ok...let me slip out of these works clothes and pop into my 'house' gear.' Rocky's rescuer disappeared up the small wooden stairs.

Hearing him rummaging about up in his bedroom, Rocky wandered about the front room. An old, antique clock ticked tocked in the corner. Scanning the sideboard, he studied the photos lined up in their separate frames. The very old black and white image in the fancy photo case showed two old people. He assumed the couple were the man's parents. The one next to it, was the photo of Rocky's rescuer. It looked like it was taken several years before. It showed the man, dressed in works clothes, resting on the crane. He could make out the smog of the iron works in the background. He wasn't what someone would call handsome, but he did have something about him.

The rest of the photos were of a woman at various ages of her life. The family resemblance was uncanny.

'Must be his sister,' Rocky found himself muttering out loud.'

A voice behind him sent a shiver up his spine. 'Did you want milk and sugar in your quite weak tea?'

'Yeah…three sugars…pleas…eeeeeeeee.' Rocky's mouth nearly dropped to the floor when he turned around. There standing bold as brass in the doorway was the man, or he thought it was the man, dressed in women's clothes. Rocky couldn't take his eyes off the deep red lipstick on the man's painted lips.

'Sorry to startle you darling,' the man said softy.

'You're…you're…Billy Bessy?' Rocky stuttered.

'Well,' the man smiled, 'it's William Cyril Morgan…but a few of the less educated people in this town refer to me by that name…yes!'

Tales of Billy Bessy were legendary throughout the borough. He was the first, well the first, openly, dressing-up transvestite the town ever had. Rumours had been rife about the old Mayor and his liking for suspenders and silky underwear, but that was never proved. There was no mistaking that with Billy when he stepped out of his closet to shock the town to its core. One night and completely out of the blue, he rocked up at the Catholic Club Christmas party in a stunning long black evening dress from Mannettes and size 11 stilettoes. No one said a word. Not even Old Miss Griffiths, who would have won the last house on the bingo before the man strutted in. People spoke in quiet whispers for months. They were shocked, they were outraged and some of them took the piss. But no one said anything to his face. Because Billy Bessy as they nicknamed him, could handle himself as well. Fight with the best of them.

'Cat got your tongue?' Billy Bessy asked. 'Did you say you wanted milk?'

'Sorry…sorry…yes, milk please.'

'Not like me…I like it black…like my men.'

'Airplane,' Rocky said.

'What?'

'Airplane.'

'Where?'

'No, the saying…I like it black like my men.' Rocky smiled. Billy looked confused. 'It's from the film, Airplane'

'Sorry darling, I've never seen it...was it good?' he asked, repositioning his false boobs. Rocky just nodded. 'Now, let's get you something to wear. Follow me.'

Rocky shadowed the man, or the woman, as he, or she, slowly mounted the stairs. Rocky could make out his shaved legs. He caught a glimpse of Billy's red silk panties as he reached the top step. Something stirred inside Rocky.

The floorboard in the bedroom creaked.

'Take your pick,' Billy motioned to the rail of grey and brown clothes hanging in a cupboard near the window. These were the clothes he wore in his day to day working life. But Rocky was already staring beyond the drabness of the everyday working man's attire. His eyes firmly fixed on the vast colours and textures of the garments hanging in the cupboard that helped turn William Morgan, crane driver into Billy Bessy, the glamourous fashion model and party planner in his spare time.

'Anything in there for me?' Rocky pointed.

'Of course. You can take your pick darling, but are you sure?'

Rocky nodded. For the first time in his life, clothes excited him. He felt thrilled. Pandora's Box had been opened into a new world. A world suddenly full of feathers, leathers, bowers, colours, hats, berets, rubber, high heels, silky underwear and corsets. His eyes nearly popped out of their sockets; his throat dry with excitement.

Billy Bessy handed him a silky slip. Nervously the boy slipped the sleek garment over his slightly brown varnished legs.

'OOOoooooooooohhhhh.' He let go of a moan. He had to think of his dad sitting in a bath of Brussel sprouts just to stop him from getting an erection. He felt like a kid in a candy shop. For the next hour, he floated about in some kinda cross-dressing heaven. Like a slightly fruity Mister Benn in a transvestite shop, he tried on garment after garment. His eyes danced and glistened. He felt as if he had risen from the dead. His world was now in techno-colour. No more black or white with grey bits. This was full-on Disney picture perfect. Rocky was reborn.

129

'It's probably best that you don't go too outrageous to start with,' Billy said. He'd had years of experience and lots and lots of abuse to back him up.

Eventually, Rocky plumped for a pair of tight orange leather trousers, a pink bower, a black, leather Dai cap, a white tee-shirt with the immortal words of Frankie Goes to Hollywood written on it, in big, bold black letters, 'Relax.'

And that's exactly what he did. He felt more relaxed than he had ever been in his entire life.

The odd couple went back downstairs. Rocky swished and twirled like a Musketeer fighting a couple of drunken Spanish soldiers. They had tea, Bessy had baked homemade scones with real cream. They sat and watched Tootsie. It was wonderful.

'Fancy the Sound of music?' Billy suggested.

Rocky nodded. There was an electricity between them. Rocky felt as if he was in heaven. He had crawled out of his personal hell. Then he leapt up. 'Oh no, my friends...I forgot about them...I've got to go...I've got to go.' Rocky turned before walking out the front door, 'I'll be back,' he tried to mimic Arnie's Austrian accent. He sounded more like Mister Grayson on helium.

Chapter 12
BREAD

'Welcome to the Gurnoz', the large sign in front of them stated in dark, blood coloured letters. Underneath it someone had scribbled, *twinned with Chuck Norris since The Way of the Dragon in 1972!*

In fact, that part was true. The place had been so rough in the 70's that Chuck Norris got invited to come over and help sort out some of the nasty elements up on the estate. But after getting beaten up three times in 35 minutes, the Kung Fu expert flew back home. 'You should see the place,' he told the air stewardess when he was safely aboard the Jumbo jet heading back to the USA, 'even the fat, ugly women in their pyjamas wanted to fight me.'

Anyway, enough of Chuck Norris, the cry baby, let's get back to the story.

'So, this is the infamous Gurnoz,' Dorothy muttered. 'It doesn't look that bad,' she added. At exactly that moment, two boys galloped passed on a horse, sprayed bright purple with spray paint.

Off into the distance, the roof of the Gurnoz shops stretched up into the gloomy skyline like an evil castle in a Disney movie.

'That's where we have to go?' Baglady grunted. Right on cue, a bolt of lightning lit up the grey sky.

Bob made the sign of the cross, five times.

'Oh my,' whispered Dorothy, 'that looks ghastly.'

From out of the alleyway, Thug Boy and his Sidekick appeared. Sidekick pushed a brand-new customized pram with flames painted on the side.

'I told the ex I didn't want to see him this weekend, see.' Drinking a can of cider, Thug Boy pointed at the baby in the pram. 'I haven't seen this one since the 4D scan.'

'How old is he now, butt?'

'About 6 or 7 months, I think.' He walked down the steps. 'Watch you don't get dog shit on the wheels.'

'Oh shit...too late.' Sidekick yelped, 'sorry.'

'You idiot.'

Dorothy pointed towards the shops. 'Ok, let's go.'

Thug boy stopped his verbal abuse towards his mate. He turned and looked at the peculiar looking gang. 'Oh...oh...oh...why are you talking so funny for?'

'Funny for?' Sidekick repeated the last few words, while curling up his top lip.

Bob whispered in Dorothy's ear.

'Oh yes, sorry.' Dorothy tried to disguise her voice, 'hi butt, we'll just looking for the wizard.'

'Which one?' replied Thug Boy.

'What?' she asked.

'I said, which wizard are you looking for?' |He rolled his eyes.

'Looking for?' the Sidekick tried his best to look mean. It failed.

'How many are there?' asked Bob.

Using his fingers, Thug boy started to count. He gave up after ten. 'There's fucking hundreds of 'em.'

'Hundreds,' copied his sidekick...again.

Bob piped up, 'What other wizards are there, maaaaaan?'

'Oh...there's the Wizard of the Spar Shop, a couple of Wizards of Pitbull's,' the Sidekick barked like a dog, 'Down boy,' Thug Boy added, 'the Wizard of the Betting Offices, the Wizards of Ma and Da tattooed on your knuckles, Roy Wood is here.'

Dorothy and Bob gave each other a quick high five.

Sidekick cried out in a loud 'Noddy Holder, from the pop group Slade, style chant, 'It's Christmassssssssss.'

'Woooo...Wooooooo.' Bob strolled over to the boy with the round NHS glasses. He grabbed the boy by the collar of his shell suit. 'Butt, you got to know your Roy Woods from your Noddy Holders.' He poked him in the chest.

'I'm only 17, butt.'

Thug Boy looked bored. 'Anyway, there's the Wizard of Shakin' Stevens, the Elvis impersonator.' For some unexplained reason, both boys did an Elvis pose, curling their lips up to the sky and placing one arm in the air. 'There's the Wizards of Wacky Baccy...the Wizard of...my Nan's Curly Purple Perm....'

Bob's eyes nearly popped out. 'Hang on maaaan, rewind, rewind...did you say...did you say...the Wizards of...of...Wacky Baccy?'

'Yep...there's loads of em.'

'Loads of em,' Sidekick chipped in.

Like an excited puppy, Bob leapt about. 'That's us sorted, come on...let's go and see the Wizards of Wacky Baccy instead...come on...come on.'

Baglady stopped him. 'No, we ain't...we need to see the Wizard of Gurnoz.'

'The Wizard of Gurnoz,' Thug Boy repeated.

'Gurnoz,' Sidekick repeated, repeated.

'Yes, the Wizard of Gurnoz,' the others repeated, and repeated, and repeated again, and again, and again. This time they unwittingly did a pose like the girls used to do in the TV show, Charlie's Angels. Thug Boy looked at each of them in turn.

'Hang, fucking, on,' Thug Boy screwed up his eyes, 'are you the filth?'

They shook their head. The Sidekick walked around the back of them. 'The God Squad then?'

'No...no.' they shook their head violently once more.

'You're ain't working for channel 4, are you?' Thug Boy growled at them, 'you're not here to make another one of those fucking Skint programmes?'

Another bolt of lightning lit up the sky.

An old woman pushing a shopping trolley, stopped. She spat on the ground, 'Channel fucking 4...scum. Coming over here, pinching our jobs and licking our women...scum, they are...scum.' She stormed off very angry.

Even though the woman was completely bonkers, she wasn't the only one to think that way. Almost everyone in the town had been outraged when Channel 4 had secretly made a film showing how fucked up the town really was. The thing was, everyone in the town knew how fucked up the town really was. That wasn't the point. What they were mad about was that someone had the cheek to come into the town and tell other people, outsiders no less, just how fucked up the town really was. Now that was hitting below the belt. Or as the Catholic priest of the time had said when he was interviewed by the Welsh News, 'If I had a pound for every time someone said to me that this town was fucked up, (the news producer had to bleep that bit), I'd have enough money to pack my bags and fuck off to Bangkok (and that bit was bleeped)...I fuckin luvs Bangkok.' (They completely deleted that part).

Back to the story.

'Well are you from Channel 4?' Thug Boy glared.

'FUCK OFF,' Baglady cried, 'we wouldn't stoop so low.'

'I don't trust you lot,' Thug Boy grabbed his Sidekick by his sleeve, 'let's go and burn a school down.' They sauntered off leaving the pram on the pavement.

'Hey...hello,' Dorothy tried to grab their attention, 'what about your baby?'

Thug Boy looked over his shoulder. 'Oh, you can have top shelf...I have another couple at home somewhere.'

'But we haven't got time to look after a baby,' Dorothy shouted. It was too late; the boys had disappeared down an alleyway.

The motley crew gathered around the pram.

'Good God,' said Bob, 'that's one ugly sprog.'

'You can't say that,' Dorothy looked shocked.

'But it's got no ears.'

'Or arms,' Rocky chipped in.

'Or legs,' Baglady added.

Dorothy looked into the buggy a little closer, 'It's got a tattoo on it...what does it say?' Bob picked it up. 'Kingsmill,' the girl added.

'And look...it's a brown one,' Rocky smiled.

Bob held it above his head. He hummed the theme tune to the lion king. They all bowed their head.

'Hang on,' voiced Baglady, 'that's not a baby...it's a loaf of fuckin' bread. What the fuck?'

'Are you sure?'

'Of course, I'm fucking sure,' Baglady shook her head. 'It's got crusts...now just put that baby...no, the bread, in the corner and let's get going.'

Thug Boy popped his head out of the alleyway. 'Oh...Oh...Oh...no one puts baby in the corner.' He walked back towards them. 'You got a problem with us, hippy boy.' He pointed at Bob. He didn't give him chance to answer. 'Is it now? Right, that's it...I'm going to get my gang.' He yelled out like a wolf who had somehow caught his nuts in an escalator in a shopping Mall.

From nowhere came the sound of catlike singing. 'We are the Gurnoz-Shop gang. the Gurnoz-Shop Gang, the Gurnoz-Shop Gang,' five boys in shiny track-suits and baseball caps, turned the wrong way around, appeared from alleyways like meat-eating zombies in a slaughterhouse. In perfect step, they aligned themselves behind Thug Boy and Sidekick without dropping a note. 'And in the name of the Gurnoz-Shop Gang. We like to welcome you all to Gurnoz-shop land.' They folded their arms in unity and gave the stare they had practiced many times in Thug Boy's Nan's house.

'Well done boys,' Thug Boy shushed under his breath.

'Fuck me,' hissed Baglady, 'it's the Backward Street Gang.'

Bob sniggered. 'You are funny.'

Baglady grinned. 'I have my moments.'

Thug Boy frowned at them. 'Funny is it, Hippy boy? How funny is this then? Now giz me your fucking moneeeeeeey.'

'And your fucking trainers,' Sidekick added.

'Good one,' Thug Boy nudged him, 'and your fucking trainers.'

Baglady stood in front of Dorothy to protect her from the mob. 'Do we look like we have any money?'

Bob shook his sandal-covered foot, 'or trainers?'

'Sidekick, you idiot,' Thug Boy snarled. 'Giz us your fags then.'

'Fags then,' Sidekick didn't miss a beat.

'We haven't got any fag...sorry,' Dorothy said. She tapped down her dress to prove her point.

'Fuck me, it's like Tesco when it's snowing. Ok...giz us your drugs?'

Baglady and Dorothy glanced at Bob. 'Drugs...drugs,' stuttered the ex-roadie, 'we haven't got any drugs...honest...truth...cross my heart.' He turned his back to them while shoving his big lump of stash in his gob. He swallowed.

'Give us back my baby then.'

'It's not a baby...it's a loaf of bread. Have it.'

'Oh no,' said Thug Boy, 'not again...where the fuck did I leave Tonka this time?'

All the gang stood around thinking (or pretending to think).

'Was it under the arches when we were sniffing glue?' replied Sidekick, 'that was some mighty strong Bostick!'

'Nah, I don't think so.'

'We must have left it in that stolen car.'

'I hope not, we fucking burnt it out.'

They all looked at each other.

'Oh, I remember now,' Thug Boy said, 'didn't I leave it in the Spar shop? Remember, I put the sprog in that rack full of Wotsits when we emptied the pram out so we could nick the booze and bread.'

'Oh yeah, we were supposed to go back for it later.'

Thug Boy shrugged, 'Oh fuck it...those Indians shop keepers will look after it...Come on, let's go back to H-Q...the toasties are on me.'

'Bags me the crusts,' one of the Gurnoz gang yelled.

Thug boy whacked him on the head, 'I'm having the fucking crusts.'

The Gurnoz-Shop gang disappeared off into the distance, humming a Justin Timberlake song in complete harmony.

Chapter 13

NUN

'Why won't anyone tell us where the wizard is?' Dorothy watched the gang disappear out of sight. Her bottom lip quivering like a jelly on a plate.

'Twat knows,' Bob replied, 'but it looks like we came a long way for nothing. '

Baglady rolled her eyes in her head. 'Don't you know why?' The other two shook their heads. 'It's easy...we ain't Gurnoz enough?'

'What?'

'It's cos we ain't Gurnoz enough,' Baglady spoke louder 'Look, if you are walking around the Gurnoz...you got to look Gurnoz...act, Gurnoz.'

Dorothy pointed at man in a white shell suit with white socks and orange crocs walking towards the betting office. 'Like him?'

'Yeah, exactly like him. See, if we don't look Gurnoz, they won't trust us.' She grabbed Terry the dog and turned to Dorothy. 'Now, stick this mutt up your dress and pretend you're up the duff.'

'What?'

'Pregnant. Now, hurry.'

'Deep breath, Terry.' Dorothy did what she was ordered to do. She looked at her bump. 'But I feel stupid.'

'Do you wanna get back to Bedlinog or what?' The girl nodded, 'just do it and start swearing and spitting and trumping now and again.' Dorothy played up to the part. Baglady looked at her, 'Pity we couldn't knock your two front teeth out and cover you in badly spelt tattoos...but I guess that will have to do.'

Baglady turned to Bob. She rummaged around in her shopping trolley and pulled out a hoodie. 'Right, put that on, pull the hood up and pretend you are a proper drug dealer.'

She didn't have to ask twice. Bob had always dreamt about being a proper drug dealer since he was 12 years of age. 'I always wanted to be a Gurnoz drug dealer.'

'Now's your chance, Huggy bloody Bear.'

'Yeah maaannnnn...wanna buy some blow or do you wanna me to pop you in the assssssssss, you mammyfucker.' Bob strutted around as if he had transformed into a black, white, black rapper.

'You talk the talk,' Baglady muttered, 'but you walk like a knob. Not too black...this ain't fucking Ely in Cardiff you know. Anyway, now where's that bloody old dancing queen gone?'

From out of the gap in the garages, Rocky strutted towards them like a New York homosexual off to see the Village People in Club X on Gay Pride Day. He even did a twirl in the middle of the road. A car nearly crashed into a lamppost. 'Get out of the road, you gay, twwwwwwwat,' a voice bellowed out from the car.

'I am, what I am,' Rocky sung at the top of his voice.

'And what he is,' Bob took over, 'is out of the closet.' Rocky poked his tongue at him. 'Have you gone mental?' Bob added. 'Who the hell are you pretending to be?'

'I'm not pretending to be anyone...This is the new me.'

'You look like Elton John's afterbirth,' Baglady shook her head.

'Oh mate,' a scruffy looking teenager materialised next to Bob, 'have you got some weed, some MDMA and some bluesy.'

Bob smiled. 'It's working...it's working. I'm a real Gurnoz drug dealer.' He turned back to the boy, 'I'll see what I can do maaaaaaan.'

The boy pulled a gun out of his belt. 'Get off my fuckin patch, scum or I'll waste you and your c**ty mates.' He placed the gun next to Bob's head. 'My family have the franchise to sell any kind of drugs from Number 23, that house with the bullet holes in the front door, right up to the smashed-up phone box near that far corner. Understand?' Bob nodded. 'I said UNDERSTAND?'

'Yeah...It's ok, I'm not really a drug deale...r.'

Baglady booted Bob in the shin. 'Sorry, Mister,' she added, 'we should have known better. We better go somewhere else.'

'And don't try and be selling any out-of-date pot noodles or chicken pasties that's all...we own those franchises as well....so beware.' He shot into the air. A pigeon landed near his feet. A rat, the size of a tabby cat, dashed out of a drainpipe and dragged the bird off for tea.

The gang shuffled off around the bend.

In a non-drug-dealer voice, Bob asked, 'Oh, Baglady...now we're in "disguise" how are we going to find the wizard...exactly?'

'Just wait,' replied Baglady, 'just wait.'

Two minutes later, a nun holding a skateboard appeared. She looked left and right before skating towards them. 'Psssh...Gurnoz gang.' She hissed, flicking the board up with her foot, before catching it with one hand.

In turn they all looked the religious woman up and down for several moments.

'Are you a nun?' Rocky walked around the woman.

'No...I'm the fuckin' penguin off Batman,' the nun tutted. 'Of course, I'm a fuckin' nun...now what are you looking for?'

Dorothy piped up, 'The Wizard.'

'Which one do you want?'

'The Wizards of Wacky Backy,' Bob retorted.

'Oh. that's easy...pick any of the red doors, on any street, just say Sister Fellatio sent you. Don't forget to mention my name...I'm on commission.'

'No,' Dorothy slapped Bob's arm, 'we want to see the Wizard of Gurnoz...Glinda sent us.'

'Oh...the Wizard of Gurnoz...Glinda sent you...well, that's different. Come on, walk this way.' The nun walked sideways across the road like a crab.

'Did you hear that?' Dorothy jumped up and down excitedly, 'we're going to see the wizard. I can go home soon.'

'And I will get a home,' said Baglady.

'And me a jo...jo...jo...fiddle,' jested Bob.

They looked at Rocky. 'I'm not exactly sure what I want yet...but I'm getting there.'

They all hugged each other.

'Oh,' the nun screamed, 'I said, walk this way.'

'Fuck it, you know what they say,' shrugged Baglady, 'when in Rome, always follow the nun with the skateboard.'

Walking like drunken crabs, they followed her through the alleyway towards the shops. She led them through the shadowy underpass, where a boy lay unconscious on the concrete floor. A needle still sticking out of his arm.

Dorothy stopped to stare at him.

'Keep walking girl...it gets far worse than that,' the nun pulled her by the arm.

The building in front of them, really should have been condemned a long, long time ago. Every window boarded up; graffiti covered every inch of wall. The whole place smelt of piss and hopelessness. They walked in. It was dismal, litter covered the floor; paint peeled off the walls.

'What the f...fu...bloody hell is this place?' Bob muttered.

'Down there?' the nun pointed to a set of stairs leading down to the basement.

'Fuck right off,' Bob spoke for all of them, 'for all we know, Leatherface could be down there waiting for us with a big machete.'

Dorothy put her hand up. 'I don't think so. I know Leatherface. He's the postman in Bedlinog.'

'Your postman? Who the fuck is your milkman?' Bob yelped, 'Dennis Neilson?'

'No, it's Ernie.' She replied.

'No way! Your milkman isn't called Ernie.'

'He is and he drives the fastest milk float in Bedlinog.'

'Fuck off,' grunted Baglady.

'He does...honest.'

The Nun coughed. 'Have you lot finished? I have other things to do you know...now down there, I said,' the nun pointed again.

Warily, they inched their way down the steps. Murky water ran down one corner of the wall. What they saw when they reached the bottom was too shocking for words. Four drug addicts lay sprawled out on the floor. A priest walked between then, covering them with blankets. The group stopped on the bottom rung of the stairs, afraid to take another step.

Dorothy was first to speak, 'Ohhh...Jiminy Cricket...what kinda place is this?'

'This is the only drug rehabilitation centre left in this entire town,' the nun answered, 'go on have a look.'

The gang of four moved amongst the chaos and the damp floor. A boy crawled across on his belly and grabbed Rocky's leg. 'Have you got any crack...or heroin...or POT...noodles?'

'Get off me.' Rocky shrieked.

'Come on Butt...I need a hit...anything.'

Rocky stuck close to Baglady. Even though she smelled like the insides of a rotten cow, the boy knew if the chips were down she would be the one to count on to get them through it. He held his nose.

'There he is,' the nun pointed.

Bob looked about. 'Who?'

'The Wizard.'

Dorothy looked confused, 'Who? The Wizard of...of...of Gurnoz.'

The nun tutted again. 'No, the Wizard of San Fran-fucking-cisco. Of course, the Wizard of Gurnoz...we're in the fuckin Gurnoz, ain't we? Fuck me, do you come with a dull-as-fuck warning sticker.' She looked at the label on the girl's dress.

'She's from Bedlinog,' Bob smirked.

'Enough said, married your first cousin yet?' the nun joked.

'No...I haven't...now get off me.' Dorothy looked at the priest and added, 'but he's...he's a priest.'

'Yeah...It's Father Wizard. Father Billy Wizard.'

Bob stopped proceedings. 'No way...you telling me that he's called...Billy Whizz...ard.' He doubled up in the corner, hands on his hips.

The priest didn't look at them. 'What do you lot want? He checked the pulse of one of the boy's stretched out on the thin mattress on the ground. Dorothy and the others shook with fear as they look about. 'Well...speak up?'

Rocky shoved Dorothy forward. 'If...If you please, I...I am Dorothy.' She looked back at the others for moral support. 'We've come to ask you for help.'

One of the drug addicts laying on the floor started to convulse. His body shook, eyes rolled in his head, a creamy substance like chicken soup dripped from the corner of his mouth. The wizard knelt down next to him. He smoothed the boy's head, while whispering in his ear.

The gang just stood staring in disbelief. Dorothy placed her hand up to her mouth to stop herself from crying out.

'Well?' the priest snapped at them.

Dorothy whispered, 'Baglady there...wants a home.' Her eyes still fixed on the poor boy struggling for breath.

'Home...has she got 7 kids?' The priest asked. They all stared at Baglady.

'What?'

'Have you got 7 kids?' asked Rocky.

'Who do you think I am? Katie fuckin' Price...course I haven't got 7 kids...I fucking hate kids.'

The priest shook his head. 'Well you ain't got much of a chance. I suggest you start knocking out a few sprogs.'

'She's 130,' Bob joshed.

Baglady flicked Bob's left nut. He doubled up again, but this time in pain. The priest pointed at the ex-Roadie. 'What about you? '

'I'm looking for a...well maybe looking for a...J...J...J...one of them things that begins with J.'

'A joint?' one of the druggy boys on the floor muttered. 'I'd love a puff now.'

'I fucking wish,' Bob licked his lips, 'Oh sorry, father...no not a joint...a...Jo...Jo...Jo....'

'A job.' Father Wizard interrupted. Bob nodded. 'Well, you can always go work up the slaughterhouse, they are always looking for bodies up there and I know the manager.'

'No way maaaaaaaan...I'm a vegetarian...meat is murder. Have you got anything with cheese?'

It was the priests turn to shake his head. 'If that's the case, I can't help you then.'

With a double cheesy grin, Bob gave him a big thumbs up.

'Uh...and you.' The man of the cloth glared at Rocky.

'Me...me...I wanna be...a...a...' the boy's words got stuck in the back of his throat.

'Well, speak up.'

Rocky tried again but nothing came out. Instead he fainted, falling backwards onto one of the drug addicts, who let out a mousey kind of shriek.

Dorothy folded her arms. 'Oh...Oh...Oh...there's no need to frighten him like that, he only wants to be an actor!'

'Actor! Actor!' The priest covered the druggie boy on the floor up with a blanket. 'This poor boy here, was going to be a professional footballer until he got addicted. Now he will have to play for Cardiff City...So go.'

'But we were told you could help us!' Dorothy muttered.

'Look about you girl...what do you see...well?'

She was going to say, a gang of weird boys with chicken soup dripping out of the corner of their mouths but thought better of it. 'Uhhmmm...people?'

'No, not just people,' a sadness rung out in his voice, 'desperate people...desperate people all looking for my help. But I'm running a centre with no funding...no money...and no future.'

One of the addicts grabbed his ankle. 'Father Wizard, we just had a letter off the council demanding that we do our own recycling now.'

'Jesus, Mary and the other one...And now...recycling...I would love to help but I can't. So, go...go I said.'

The crew slowly walked back up the steps. Dorothy turned back She had other ideas. She ran back to him.

'Well, Father Billy Wizard,' she added. Behind them, Bob burst out laughing again. She turned and glared at him.

'Sorry, I can't help it,' Bob shrugged, 'it's just so fuc...fuc...just so funny. Billy Whizz...sorry father.'

Dorothy continued, 'can we help you, father?'

Father Wizard's tone softened a little. 'It would help if you could stump up some cash since our funding's been slashed.'

Dorothy glanced around the room again. The scene still wasn't any easier on the eye. The shells of teenagers lay about the place. Their bodies longing for its next fix. She could see that they had no life in their eyes and no spark left in their limp bodies. Like the human equivalent of a pack of stolen cars which had been driven around at full speed before being burnt out and abandoned on the mountainside. 'But who would stop your funding?' she enquired.

'I'll tell you who. The Wicked Bitch of the Council,' the priest replied. All the drug addicts started booing, 'that's who...she wants this place shut down.'

'Maybe we'll go and ask her to give your funding back,' Dorothy said proudly.

The priest laughed. Others joined in. even the boy who Dorothy thought was stone dead chuckled to himself. 'You ain't from around here are you girl?' Father Wizard added.

'No, I'm from Bedlinog...its way over that way.' She pointed in completely the wrong direction. Father Wizard moved her arm to point the right way. 'Oh, I see...it's over that way.'

'I know where it is...but this ain't no backwater little village here...This is Merthyr...the capital of corruption...the town of tyrants...the den of iniquity.' He paced around the room.'

'Maybe we could change her mind.'

'Yeah and if you aunt had bollocks she'd be your uncle.' The priest made his point with a humourless statement.

'You know her, do you?' Bob laughed.

'Funny Bob,' Dorothy glared at him. 'But Mister Wizard...if we get you funding, will you help us?'

'I like your spirit girl...but the only way you would get money out of the Wicked Bitch is if you killed her.'

Outside, another clap of thunder shook the skies.

'Kill her!' Dorothy repeated.

'That's the way it works in this town...its dog eat dog.'

Terry gulped.

The Match of the Day jingle from an Ice Cream van filled the air. Like flesh-eating zombies, all the drug addicts got up and staggered towards the exit. 'Bloody hells, bloody bells,' the priest yelled, 'it's Druggie Bell, the biggest drug and ice-cream dealer in the town...I'll never get them back now.'

One of the addicts turned to another and muttered, 'Lend us a quid butt, I want a 99 with some MDMA sprinkled on the top.'

'I'm having an oyster shell covered in spice...I need a good fix.'

Dorothy watched the last of them shuffle out of the building. She turned back to the priest. 'We better kill her then Mister Wizard.' She held out her hand for a high five. The priest took her hand and shook it.

'Good luck,' he muttered.

Chapter 14

HORSE

'Let's do it. Let's do it now,' Baglady pumped her fist in the air as they walked out into the greyness of the afternoon. 'Let's go kill the Wicked Bitch of the Council.' The old woman stopped dead in her tracks. The sign from the Gurnoz Social club flickered brightly in the distance like a beacon on top of a lighthouse. 'Hang on a little minute...maybe we can have a quick drink first...just one...like?'

'NO!' Dorothy shrieked on seeing the beaten-up old sign of the rundown social club. The place looked worse than she expected it to look. All of the windows boarded up to protect it from vandals. The front door covered in metal plate to stop thirsty drunks kicking the panels in at nine o clock in the morning. The peddle-dashed walls of the club mixed with badly spelt graffiti made it look like a large corn-flake box created by a trendy, dyslexic designer. 'Glinda, warned me never to go to there.'

'Only cos she's banned for fighting,' Baglady licked her lips, 'come on, one drink won't harm...and Terry looks like he needs some water.'

Rocky clapped his hands, 'Oh yesssss, we must go in...look, quick...quick...its karaoke tonite.' He bounced up and down on the balls of his feet, 'Bags me singing Gloria Gaynor...I will survive,' he bellowed out.

Still trying his best to act like a Gurnoz drug baron, Bob shrugged his shoulders and grunted, 'any black rapper for me...like that cool Eminem motherfucker.'

Stern-faced Baglady reminded them all, 'but don't forget, we're from the Gurnoz...ok...so we've got to act Gurnoz...be Gurnoz.'

They all nodded.

'I said, OK?'

'Yes.' said Rocky.

'For fuck sake, it's not "yes"...it's yeah, bitch. You sound more like an Eton school boy. So?'

They looked at her.

'Well?'

'Well, what?'

'Well, say it.'

'Say what?'

'Say, yeah Bitch?'

'But we know,' said Bob.

'Just say it.'

'Ok...all together now,' Bob counted to three. 'Yeah, you ugly, smelly Bitch.'

'I'm warning you Bob,' Baglady mocked, 'that wasn't so fucking hard was it.'

They all took a deep breath and strolled in through the doors. The pong was the first thing to hit Dorothy. The place whiffed like a giant ashtray which someone had poured some beer into and then left on a hot radiator. It reeked. Fist holes and blood stains peppered the flocked wallpaper. A line of fruit machines bleeped away in the foyer. In front of them, women in slippers with hair in curlers fed the hungry contraptions nonstop with pound coins.

'This is worse than that basement,' Dorothy whispered.

Everything in the room stopped when the gang walked in to the main hall. Eyes glared at them with suspicion. All the men looked and acted as if they were living in a cowboy movie. Dozens and dozens of beer-bellied John Waynes in flared trousers with huge moustaches that made Magnum PI's facial bush look scrawny than Hitler's own attempt. The men sat around tables, playing cards and drinking warm beer while smoking rollies.

The Gurnos-shop gang stood by the bar, trying their best to look hard. All dressed the same in their purple and white shells suits and baseball caps turned the wrong way around. The only difference being the different sized gold chains around their necks. The thicker the gold chain, the higher up in the gang one was.

A woman with jet black, dyed hair staggered onto the stage. Microphone in one hand, a half empty bottle of Newcastle Brown in the other. 'Come on you bunch of fuckin' muppets...let's have you. We've got all of your favourites here tonight. Cefn, must be missing an angel. Sweet Home Aberaman, and my favourite, I love the sound of Mountain Ash.'

Thug Boy and Sidekick sauntered in. Between them they held a big, blue recycling bag full of knocked off stuff.

'Oh mam...switch that off a sec,' Thug Boy cried out at the top of his voice. She lowered the music. 'Now listen up everyone,' Thug Boy walked down between the rows of tables, yelling. 'Listen up,' I said, 'I have some right bargains for you lot.' He reached into the bag. 'First off, I've got Drrrruuuuggggsssss...everything you want...dope, speed, uppers, downers, bombers, dexys, purple hearts...I have blues...Father's Day is coming up...so why don't you get dad hard...with some extra strength Viagra. Half a tab and he could knock a fucking nail in the wall after popping one of these beauties, let me tell you.'

A 76 old woman shouted out, 'Give me 10 of the bastards...I have a few picture frames to hang and some hanging baskets.' Everyone laughed.

Thug Boy clambered up on the tables in the middle row. People moved their drinks as he sauntered towards the stage. 'I have a few prescription books, fake passports, genuine Monster Munch crisps...and some of the dirtiest cock books you can imagine.'

'Like what?'

'How does...Clitty, Clitty, Bang, Bang, grab you Miss Brown?'

'I'll have one and have you got anything with some big, black cock in it?' she asked.

Thug Boy rummaged about in the bag. 'I've got Black Beauty...the 12-inch uncut version.'

'Ooohhhhh...I can feel my dam walls ready to burst just thinking of it.' She rushed over, a tenner gripped in her hand. Pretty soon, a crowd of people surrounded Thug Boy like kids waiting in line to see Santa in Asda on Christmas Eve.

Bob, Dorothy and Baglady sat around a small table up near the women's bogs. It wasn't the best place to sit for various reasons.

'I wonder if he' got any hash on him,' Bob was stopped from going over by Baglady.

'Just drink and behave,' she instructed.

'Can't we go now,' Dorothy finished the last drop of her lemonade, 'we've been here for an hour.'

'Hang on a sec...let me finish me cider,' protested the tramp. She had already knocked back 6 pints in that time.

'But there's an old guy standing over there, glaring at me.' They all turned around.' NO! Don't look. He's just staring...he must have some big car keys in his pockets 'cos he's playing with them a lot.'

Baglady slyly turned around. She turned back. 'Oh, don't worry about him. That's only Arthur the pervert...he's harmless enough...unless he's got you tied to his bed in the attic where his dead mother sleeps.'

'What?' the girl screeched out in shock.

'Only joking,' Baglady laughed, 'the beds in the cellar.'

Bob wasn't listening. He smoked his joint. The smoke merged with the rest of the fag smoke swirling around the room. It was so thick;

the discoloured ceiling tiles couldn't be seen unless someone had a gas mask and goggles on. And even then, they would struggle.

Rocky raced up through the crowd towards them. 'Come on, come on...we're on.'

'On what?' Baglady burped. Her rancid breath polluted the already smoke-polluted air.

'The karaoke,' Rocky clapped his hands, 'God, have you been eating pickled eggs?'

'No, I bloody haven't,' Baglady tried to smell her own breath, 'anyway, there's no bloody way I'm doing that. I can't sing.'

'Same as the rest of them in here,' Rocky grinned, 'they all sound like cats stuffed in carrier bags and thrown in the Doggy Lake. So, come on,' he grabbed their hands, 'let's show them what proper singing is all about.' They looked at him. 'It will be a laugh...come on.' He led them to the screen on the stage. Bob staggered. He was so stoned he didn't know what the hell was going on. He stood facing the opposite way. 'Are we queuing up for chips?' he nudged Dorothy.

'Fuck me,' said the woman running the sound system, 'and now we have the cast from the Wizard of Oz.' She sniggered, smoke escaped from her nose, and her ears!!

Everyone in the room laughed. Well, all except Arthur the pervert who had his eyes closed and was ejaculating into a pint glass. He finished, wiped his hands in the curtains and retired to the snooker room for a cigar. The pint glass sat on the bar.

'Right, we're ready,' Rocky rocked back and forth. Excitement pumping through his veins.

The music started. The aggressive acoustic guitar strains of 'That's Entertainment' by the Jam blasted out of the speakers. The words appeared on screen. Rocky started singing, the rest joined his lead.

'A police car and a screamin' siren, Pneumatic drill and ripped-up concrete, Baby bread wailing, a stray dog howling, The screech of brakes and lamplight blinking'

No one needed to read the screen for the words to the popular chorus. The song had been something of an anthem in the town since it came out in 1980. Everyone to a man, screamed out, *'That's Merthyr Tydfil, That's Merthyr Tydfil.'*

It was the sacred song adopted by the town. Women jumped up onto the table. Dancing like it was 1999. By the second verse, the gang's confidence had grown sky high. Even Baglady joined in. The words which appeared on the screen had been doctored to fit the violence which walked around the High Street of the town, in big, 11-hole bovver boots, looking for a fight

'A kick in the balls and a kick in the balls, A kick in the balls and a kick in the balls, A kick in the balls and a kick in the balls, A kick in the balls and a kick in the balls,'

Rocky grabbed the mic. 'Hello GURNWAH...are you ready? 1...2...a 1...2....3...4...*I said that's Merthyr Tydfil...That's Merthyr Tydfil...La la la la la, ah La la la la la, ah.'*

The crowd belted it out. One table collapsed under the weight of three 'big boned' women jumping up and down. One of them screamed after she thought someone had nicked her chicken wings. At the back, someone slid Alan the midget across the bar. He landed head first in a rubbish bin, his little legs kicking wildly about like a beetle on heat. On the stage, Dorothy pogoed up and down like Sid in the Roxy club in '77. But unlike Sid, she forgot she had Terry the dog hidden under her dress. All of a sudden, the dog tumbled onto the wooden sprung flooring. At the same time, Bob's hoodie fell down off his face.

'Hang on,' yelled Thug Boy, holding a stolen sky dish in his hand, 'I've seen them before...they ain't fucking Gurnoz!'

'KILL EM,' an old woman bellowed.

'STRING EM UP,' another voice rose up from another corner of the room.

The karaoke queen walked slowly to the edge of the stage, 'Eat their kidneys and feed them to the fuckin' dogs,' she sung in time to the music.

Dorothy and the others backed up into the corner. Sadly, for them, it was the wrong corner. The corner opposite to them had a fire escape leading to the car park. Unfortunately, the one they found themselves cornered in was a complete dead end. The biggest dead end in the history of dead ends.

Thug Boy and his gang scurried towards them. One held a flick knife, another a club with nails sticking out of it. They inched forward like a pack of hyenas but with a lot less intelligence.

Thug boy couldn't believe his luck. He'd been waiting for an occasion like this for months, or even years. An incident where he could show off how good the dance skills of his homemade crew were. He stood in front of his gang. 'Hang on...hang on now boys...let's get in positions.' He waited until the other six of them, in matching shell suits, moved to form some kind of arrow head shape. 'No...no...Lenny James...what did we practice.' Thug Boy rolled his eyes, and put his hand on his hip, 'you on the left, not the right. There, go there. Right, boys...now big snarl on your faces, shoulders back, stomachs tucked in...right, click your finger and...wait for it...right,' he changed his voice, a lot deeper, 'It's West Side Story, boys.'

The gang clicked their fingers and danced across the dancefloor in front of the stage like the Jets in the musical movie. Just in front of Dorothy, Thug Boy did the splits. Landing spread eagled on the deck. He sat leg's wide apart on the dirty floor. He waited for a few seconds, agony written all over his face. 'Help me fucking up, boys.'

Two of them got him to his feet. They stood in front of Dorothy and her gang.

Dorothy stepped forward. 'Hello...I'm Dorothy We're here to help you.'

'How?' Thug Boy said, a little higher than normal.

'We are going to see the Wicked Bitch to get you funding,' she replied.

Thug Boy looked at them suspiciously. 'Funding, for what?'

'To help the Wizard and his drug centre,' Baglady piped up.

'Not bad,' Thug Boy voiced his approval, 'but what else?'

'What else do you want more money for?' asked Dorothy.

'Drugs,' muttered Bob.

'Shut up, Bob.'

Thug Boy took off his cap. 'I'll tell you what we want...I'll tell you now. We want new Burberry baseball hats.' He pointed to the boy next to him, 'and real zip up Bench hoodie jackets.' He moved across the line of youths to a boy covered in gold chains. 'And more gold chains for Lenny here.' He shook his head and pointed at the white shell suit trackee bottoms another one of his gang members had on. 'And a few more of whatever the fuck he's wearing.' He looked to his left, 'Beanie hats for the winter and a couple of 9 carat gold rings.'

'9 carat gold rings,' his Sidekick repeated.

Thug boy grabbed Sidekick by the collar. He eyeballed him. 'You repeat my words again and I'll stick that ring up your arse.'

When he turned back, Sidekick cried, 'up my arse.'

Thug boy carried on. 'We want more betting offices...Offies...and definitely, simpler ways to do our recycling.'

Dorothy smiled. 'I promise you...there will be a simpler recycling system that everyone can understand.'

Recycling was one of Bob's bug bears. 'Yeah...and two blue bags maaaaaan...and more green containers and colour coded plastic stuff. Wicked.' He high fived the Thug Boy.

'Hurray for Dorothy,' Thug Boy muttered. Everyone in the club started chanting, 'Dorothy...Dorothy...Dorothy.'

Back in her office, the Wicked Bitch sat on her throne, her face like thunder. A little bird had told her about the terrible rumours coming out of the estate. 'Uprising,' she bellowed down the phone at one of her snitchers, 'and they want to do what.'

'More money your highness.'

'More money, off me! I'll show them. Who are the ring leaders?' the snitch mentioned a girl with a dog and her weird-looking mates. 'Are they now? Well we'll see about that.' She hung up the phone and dialled another number.

'Come on...come on...answer the bloody thing.' In her temper she snapped a pencil between her fingers.

The soft tones of the woman's voice on the automated answering machine on the other end seeped like a gas through the telephone line. 'If you want to hire a hit man, press 1...if you are calling about knee capping a neighbour or a relative, press 2. beheading, 3, castration, 4, knitting classes, 5 or hang on for the assistance.'

The music to Greensleeves played.

'I'll fucking Greensleeves you,' the Bitch grunted.

'HELLO,' a man in a thick, Welsh accent finally answered.

'At last...right...' The Bitch butted in.

'Who is it please?'

'It's me...your fucking boss...now shut up and listen. There's a situation taking place up on the Gurnoz...I want it sorted.'

'When?'

'Fucking now.'

'But we're going on my lunch break in 5 minutes, mun.'

'Never mind, your fucking lunch break. I want it sorted NOW! And bring me the ringleaders.' She slammed the phone down again.

Back in the Gurnoz club, the frenzied crowd were all still chanting. 'DOROTHY, DOROTHY, DOROTHY,' when a high-pitched, piercing sound off in the distance broke their concentration.

Chapter 15
TOYS R US

The first strains of the police sirens could be heard from the road leading into the estate. First there was silence in the packed hall, followed by a lot of pulling of faces and then as the sirens got nearer and nearer, complete and utter bedlam.

'It's the fuckin' pigs,' an old woman screamed out. Clutching a handful of Viagra tablets and two porno movies. She ran across several tables before diving headfirst out of a window.

Scared shitless, people raced off in all directions. Pockets and arms carrying dope, cocaine, guns, knives, porn films, stolen kettles and bags of new potatoes (they too had been stolen, but not from the same place as the kettles.)

'It's the pigs,' Bob grunted, 'quick Dorothy...we've got to get outta here.'

'Pigs, like animal pigs?'

'No, you in-bred, the Coppers, the filth, the scum, the rozzers, the fuzz, the bow-street runners' Dorothy still looked confused. 'The police...it's the fucking police.'

'But maybe they will help us?' she flashed her white teeth into a cute smile.

'Yeah,' Baglady piped up from up near the emergency exit, 'and like the wizard said, if your Aunt had bollocks she'd be your Uncle. Now

Dorothy, stop being so bloody nice and trusting and grow some balls yourself...and run...NOW.'

Baglady and Rocky disappeared like rats down the fire escape.

Dorothy refused to budge. She had a stubborn streak in her at times.

'Please yourself.' Bob disappeared as well.

The hall in the club stood silent and deserted, except for the girl and her pet dog. Two minutes later, the already battered old front doors to the establishment, burst open. Two Coppers sauntered in. Both overweight, both going bald and both looking like two twats from Twatville with first-class honours degrees in 'how to be a twat' and with only one thing on their small-town, racist minds, twattacussing someone.

'Hello...hello...hello...what have we got here?' the younger, and fatter, of the two Coppers muttered.

'Mister Policeman...I'm Dorothy, and this is my dog Terry, I wonder if you can help us to right a great injustice?'

The other Copper, the Sergeant, held out his hand to stop her talking. 'Have you got a licence for that brute?' he hissed and bent his knees at the same time.

'Terry is not a brute...and no I haven't...we don't need one in Bedlinog.'

A smirk crawled up the Sergeant 's face. 'But this ain't fucking Bedlinog, darling.'

The other Copper slyly took something out of a plastic bag and planted its contents on the floor near the fruit machine. 'Look Serge...fowling in a public place...that's a criminal offence.'

Dorothy looked at the large lump of poo in horror. 'I can assure you that Terry didn't do that. He's fully house trained.'

The Sergeant shook his head slowly. 'We didn't say it was the dog...you're nicked, darling.'

The younger Copper handcuffed the girl and the dog and dragged them outside into the car park. Headfirst, they got chucked into the back of the waiting Black Mariah. As the van pulled away, people popped out from doors, windows, wheelie bins and underneath cars.

'I fuckin' hates the filth, me,' yelled the nun. With murder in her eyes, she booted a stray cat up onto the roof of a garage.

Three miles away, and securely locked behind security fencing, Dorothy sat at the table in the white tiled police cell. Behind her, the Coppers argued like a married couple trying to decide who should hold the TV remote control on a Saturday night.

'But it's my turn to be the bad cop, Sarge.'

'It's not...you were the bad cop last week, remember.' The other cop shook his head, 'you do...you beat that Lolly-pop woman up. Remember?'

'Oh yeah.' The Copper clutched his fist and smirked, 'that was a good one. Still unconscious as well I heard. I've been nominated for the "truncheon bash of the month" award. I hope I win it this year.'

The Sergeant walked over to the table, 'So it's my turn now.' He knelt down, his face the same height as the girl. 'Ok scum...where did you hide the diamonds?'

'What?'

'The fucking South African diamonds, scumbag.'

'What South African diamonds?' Dorothy looked at him.

'Don't give us that...now tell us or we'll...we'll,' he looked her up and down, 'or, we'll...we'll...hide your shoes.'

'Sarge, mun,' the other cop chipped in, 'see...no wonder I should be bad cop...you are useless...How will hiding her shoes help solve the case?'

The Sergeant wasn't sure, but he wasn't going to be made a fool of in front of a prisoner. 'Cos...cos...cos...she wouldn't be able to run away then, would she?'

'Good point.' With one eye fixed on the girl, the other cop started to take her left shoe off.

Suddenly, the door to the cell crashed open. It nearly fell off its hinges. The Wicked Bitch entered like a baddie in a Kid's pantomime. If she had a moustache, that would have been the perfect moment to twiddle the end of it and cackle with laughter.

Both Coppers straightened up. In perfect harmony, both clicked their heels and made Nazi salutes. Terry barked.

'Leave those shoes alone,' she demanded. She stared at the girl. 'Well...well...well...so we meet again and this time, I heard you want some money off me?'

'Yes...yes,' Dorothy's spirits lifted, 'money to help the poor souls in the Gurnoz.' The Wicked Bitch paced in front of her. 'And Wicked Bitch...can you help me please...these men...said...I had a poo in the hall in the social club...and I didn't...I wouldn't do that...I...'

'Ych Y Fi,' The Bitch scrunched up her features, 'that's disgusting. Defecation...as well as stealing. We have a right hardened criminal here, boys.'

'I told you she stole the South African diamonds,' the Sergeant beamed, 'didn't I?'

'I haven't stolen anything.'

'Not the diamonds,' the Wicked Bitch moved in closer to her. 'She stole my shoes.'

'I didn't.'

The Wicked Bitch wrestled one of the shoes off Dorothy's feet. She handed it to the younger Copper. 'Read what it says on there?'

He pulled his glasses out of his top pocket. 'Size...9 and half. Bloody hell you got big feet for a woman.'

Before the Wicked Bitch could say anything, in the opposite corner, the Sergeant interrupted. 'You know what they say about a woman with big feet, don't you?' Again, he bent his knees in a way a Copper would do in a Carry-on movie.

Even Dorothy and Terry, outsiders in this world, knew that wasn't the right thing to say.

The Wicked Bitch stomped over to the Sergeant. He stood shivering in his police issue boots. 'No...I don't,' she hissed into his face like she was blowing cigarette smoke in a 1950's fag advert. 'Tell me?'

'Hummm,' the Sergeant 's voice dried up in his throat, 'big feet, hummm...hummm...big...brain.'

'Better be.' She spun around, pointing at the other policeman, 'Read the other part...idiot.'

'Oh...right mam,' he checked again, 'these, white stilettoes, belong to the Wicked Bitch of the Council and if you see them on anyone else that means they have stolen them.' The Wicked Bitch snarled. 'Oh...Oh...Oh,' added the Copper, 'look, there's a photo of Donald Trump in the heel.'

'Oooooh let me see...let me see,' the other policeman bounded over.

Dorothy folded her arms. 'I didn't steal them...someone gave them to me.'

'That's a lie...who would give you my shoes?'

At that exact moment, as if it had been staged, Glinda from Hing Hongs got pushed into the room by another fat, balding Copper who really was the king of the cop twats. 'Get your dirty, fucking paws off me, PC Blod...or I'll have you for sexual harassment.'

Dorothy pointed. 'She did. She gave me the shoes...honest....tell them, Glinda...please.'

'Sorry love,' Glinda held up her hand, 'I'm not telling them fuck all. I have enough on my plate. They've already accused me of shooting the Mayor's wife and pissing in the soup.'

'You did shoot the Mayor's wife,' the arresting officer interjected.

'Yeah, I told her she was banned...but I didn't piss in the soup...that was Elvis Shaky Lee the cook.' Everyone in the room except the Wicked Bitch and Dorothy did some sort of Elvis pose and curled up their top lip. Even Terry the dog got involved.

'Stop fucking doing that,' the Bitch demanded. She pointed at the police officers. 'You three, I want a word.' The Coppers followed her to the back of the room, where a lot of whispering, poking and prodding with her truncheon took place.

Glinda sidled up to Dorothy, 'Hide this for me, love...quick.'

'A gun!'

Glinda puffed out her cheeks. 'No, it's a fucking onion bhaji. Of course, it's a fuckin' gun...now Schhh...stop being all nicey nice and hide it.'

Dorothy did what she was told. The weapon was positioned neatly up her dress.

The Wicked Bitch and the Coppers came back.

'Dorothy, where are the rest of your gang?' the Bitch asked.

'I haven't got a gang.'

'You do.'

'I don't.'

'Oh yes, you do.'

'Oh no, I don't.'

'Oh yes, you do.'

'Oh no, I...don't.'

'Fucking hell,' Glinda piped up, 'this sounds like an Owen fuckin' Money pantomime. I half expect Madam Twanky to walk in here holding a magic dildo'

'Wicked Bitch,' the Sergeant said, 'ask her about the diamonds?'

'What?'

'The South Africa diamonds that were stole from Ron the Italian.'

'Ron the Italian...I thought he was dead.' asked the younger Copper.

'Who? Ron the Italian?' the Sergeant questioned.

'Yeah...Ron the Italian!'

'No, that's Ron the Milkman.'

'What? Ron the Milkman is dead!'

'Yeah.'

'When did that happen?'

'A week ago. He got shot!'

'Ron the Milkman got shot?'

'Yeah.'

'By who?'

'Ron the Italian, apparently.'

'Fuck off! Ron the Milkman shot Ron the Italian?'

'Straight through the head.'

'Because of the South African diamonds?'

'No, cos Ron the Milkman was pegging Ron the Italian's wife while he was away in South Africa.'

BANG

The Wicked Bitch's truncheon nearly snapped the desk in half. 'I don't give a fuck if Ron the Milkman was pegging Ron the Italian's dog...now....'

'He hasn't got a dog.'

'Who?'

'Ron the Italian, he's allergic to them. Anyway, ask her about Ron's South African diamonds.'

'I thought he owned an Alsatian,' the younger Copper asked.

'Who?'

'Ron the Italian.'

'No, that was Ron the pipefitter.'

'Oh yeah.'

The Wicked Bitch smacked the one cop across the head. He fell to the ground. Little police helicopters circled around his brain. 'The next one to mention anyone called fucking Ron will get hit...very, very hard.'

'You just hit him,' the Sergeant hissed, 'very, very hard.'

'That was a smack, not a hit...anyway, let's get back to the criminal, shall we?'

Dorothy spoke up. 'I don't know anything about any South African diamonds...honest.'

'She does...I can see by the way her eyes move to the left.'

The other Copper, still standing, looked over at him. 'Oooohhh,' he said in a pretend girly voice, 'look at Colombo. He can tell by the way her eyes move to the left.'

'Will you lot behave or I'll get you walking the beat...in Penrhys in the Rhondda...after dark.' The Wicked Bitch spun around on her heels. 'Now, last time my girl...where's your fuckin' gang?'

'I don't know.'

'Ok...I didn't want to get rough...but you left me with no choice.' She looked at the dog sitting scared under the table. 'Hold that mutt out, boys.'

'Who?'

'You lot. Hold the dog out.'

'What if he bites?' said the younger Copper.

'Yeah,' said the Sergeant, 'it's probably got rabies or an STD.'

All the Coppers moved away.

The Wicked Bitch grabbed one Copper by his hair. 'He doesn't bite as hard as me. Now hold him out.'

In a firm grip, the Coppers held the dog out by his four legs like they were about to give him the bumps. The animal's belly faced the ceiling. The Wicked Bitch pulled a switchblade out of the bag. 'I wonder how many doggie chops I could get out of this little mutt.' She pretended to shave with the deadly instrument. The cold, sharp blade slid across her bare cheek.

'No,' Dorothy tried to move, but the third Copper held her tight in the chair. 'TERRY!' she yelled again.

The Wicked Bitch pulled a hair from one of the Copper's heads and sliced it in half using the weapon. 'Now, are you going to spill the beans, or am I going to spill doggy blood?'

'Watch my uniform, I only just had it cleaned.' The Sergeant grinned.

The Wicked Bitch pressed a button on her mobile phone. *Stuck in the Middle with You* by *Stealers Wheel* played loudly. The Wicked Bitch danced like the thug in the movie, *Reservoir Dogs*. She didn't miss a beat. The Coppers looked at her in admiration.

'You should go on Strictly next year,' Glinda yelled out, 'you would fuckin' win it hands down.'

The Wicked Bitch smiled and blushed slightly. For the first time in a long, long time, she showed just a glimpse of humanity, a hint of compassion. Then she whispered in Dorothy's ear, 'I'm going to cut this doggy's lipstick off and feed it to my fish.' Humanity and compassion lost yet again.

'Don't harm Terry...please,' Dorothy begged.

Terry barked. In dog language it translated to, 'please don't cut my dick off...anything but my wax remover.'

The dog's sorrowful whimpers got drowned out by the music and the three Copper's joining in to the chorus like the backing singers in Stevie Wonder's band. With the evilest grin the Coppers had ever seen, the Wicked Bitch closed in on the poor dog, switchblade glistening in her bony fingers.

Dorothy jumped to her feet. The handgun held surprisingly steady in her outstretched hand. 'Oh...Wicked bitch,' she said confidently, 'I said, NO!'

The Wicked Bitch stopped her assault on Terry.

'Thank fuck for that,' Terry barked again.

The Bitched laughed. 'You...you are too nice...You don't have the bollocccckkkks.'

'I do.'

'Oh no, you don't.'

'Oh, yes I do.'

'For fuck sake,' Glinda shouted, 'let's not go down this route again, is it?'

The Bitch walked towards the girl. 'Now sweetie...give me the gun.'

The first shot missed its target. It smashed the one-way mirror at the far end of the room. Behind the glass stood Bob, Baglady and Rocky.

'What are you lot doing here?' cried the Bitch.

'We've come for our girl,' Baglady puffed out her chest.

'Is it. Well, after I sort her and her dog out, I'm going to get my boys to cut you three into small pieces and feed you all to my fish.'

'Fuck me,' whispered the younger Copper, 'what fish as she got? Fucking jaws.'

'She must have a big goldfish bowl.'

The Coppers started giggling.

The Bitch glared at them. She turned to face Dorothy. 'Now give me that gun, girl or else?'

The second bullet didn't miss its target. The slug ripped into the Wicked Bitch's arm, sending her crashing into the back wall. Everyone stood in silence. Even the Wicked Bitch couldn't believe it. Dorothy fired again. The next bullet journeyed through her left leg. The Wicked Bitch staggered backwards. She fell over the desk onto the floor. Dorothy stood over her and fired about hundred rounds into her.

'Where did you get that gun from?' the Sergeant asked.

'Argos,' replied Glinda.

'That was a fuckin' bargain. I better put an order in for a few dozen tomorrow.'

'Oh, we are getting guns,' one Copper cried. They all danced about.

The Wicked Bitch twitched. The Sergeant shrieked. Dorothy sprayed her twice more. Everyone looked at her in surprise and more than a trace of respect. The girl blew on the barrel, placed her foot on the belly of the dying woman and said, 'Who says, I'm too nice?'

The Baglady and Rocky rushed into the room. 'You killed her...you killed the Wicked Bitch of the Council.'

Bob staggered in a few seconds later. 'Fuck a duck.' He blew a dope smoke ring the size of a car tyre, 'she really did it.'

'Yes,' said the Sergeant, 'and she's going down for murder for a very, very, very, long time...and you lot, are all going down with her for being accomplices...and you,' he pointed at Glinda, 'for pissing in the soup.'

'It wasn't fuckin' me...it was Elvis Shaky Lee the cook, I'm telling you.'

They all did the Elvis thing again.

'Will you stop doing that?' the Wicked Bitch croaked.

Dorothy shot her again.

'Now,' added the Sergeant, 'handcuff them all...and take them all to Cardiff nick.'

'What about the dog?' the younger Copper asked.

'Take that as well.

'What are they going to do with a dog in Cardiff nick?'

'I don't know...probably bum it in the showers same as the other new fish.'

Dorothy looked at the policeman in horror. Terry shrugged his little doggy shoulders. In his mind, he thought, 'Well, my mother always told me to try everything once...or three times!'

'No,' shouted Dorothy.'

'Hang on a minute, Dorothy,' Terry yapped, 'I bet it's not that bad, especially if I grease myself up.' His eyes glistened; his lipstick glowed bright red.

The Sergeant sighed loudly, his stomach rumbled. 'Ok...take it around the back and shoot the scabby little mutt.'

'NO!' Dorothy yelled even louder.

'Ok, boss.' The younger Copper pushed them towards the door. Terry barked.

'NO!' Dorothy reached for the gun. She pointed it at the Copper. 'Put Terry down.'

The Copper grinned. 'You can't fool us...you can't have any more bullets left.'

'Are you sure about that?'

Beads of sweat dripped off the policeman's head. He took a deep breath. 'Yeah...I...think...Yeah...definitely...or maybe...well...I'm doing it.'

'You gave me no choice.' Dorothy pressed the trigger. Everyone dived for cover. The gun didn't go off. It jammed.

'You are going to pay for that.' The Copper squeezed his hands around poor Terry's throat.

'Leave him go...please...please.'

The Copper laughed, a foul, horrible, bastard of a laugh.

'Borrow this,' Glinda slowly pulled a machine gun from under her dress. She threw it to Dorothy.

'Where the hell did you get that gun from?' the Sergeant asked.

'Toys R Us.'

'Another fuckin' bargain.'

'Yeah, it was in the for-sale bucket as well.'

Dorothy pointed the weapon at the officer. 'Hey motherfucker, let me introduce you to my little friend. Now put my dog down, boy.' The Copper did as she instructed.

'Fuck me, Dorothy,' Baglady muttered, 'you've turned into the fuckin' Terminator.'

'I'll be back,' joked one of the Coppers while walking around like a robot.

Not understanding the joke, Dorothy shot him in the leg, shattering his kneecap and sending him wriggling around in agony.

'Oooohhhhhh,' the Witch Bitch moaned.

'Arrgghhhhhhhh, she still alive,' Rocky screamed. 'Shoot her again Dorothy...shoot her again.'

Everyone in the room, including the Coppers hid behind Dorothy.

'Go on shoot the bitch,' the Sergeant cried.

Dorothy aimed the gun. 'Hang on...I nearly forgot. Hey, Mister Policeman hand me your pad please.'

The Copper handed her his notebook. Dorothy talked to herself as she wrote. 'I, the Wicked Bitch, agree to give Father Wizard all the funding he needs...forever...and ever...and ever.' She bent down to the Wicked Bitch. 'Sign it.'

'Never.'

'Sign it and I may let you live.' Dorothy unlocked the safety catch and pointed at the woman on the floor.

The Wicked Bitch reluctantly signed it. Dorothy placed the weapon between her knees and took the pad back.

BRRRRRRRRRRRRR.

The gun seemed to have a mind of its own, well with a bit of help from Dorothy accidently squeezing the trigger with her thigh. A series of bullets ripped through the Wicked Bitch's arm, nearly cutting it clean off at the elbow. With the weapon out of control, Dorothy accidently shot and killed Glinda and one of the Coppers.

'Put the fucking safety catch back on, love,' Bob yelled out from behind a bin. The tip of his joint blown off by a stray bullet.

'You killed her...you killed the Wicked Bitch of the Council, again! Ding dong, the Wicked Bitch is finally dead,' the Sergeant yelled out.

Bob staggered towards her, looking at the tip of his joint in disbelief. He struggled to speak. 'Ohhhhhhhh...what a waste? But at least, that bitch is dead.'

'Yes, she is,' the Sergeant whispered, 'and if you help bury her in the backyard, you can all go free cos I'm starving and I didn't have my dinner, and the chippie closes in 20 minutes.'

'Really?' asked Baglady.

The Copper nodded. 'It will save us with all that paperwork...I hate when someone gets killed. Worst part of the job. On my life, I went through 6 biros when Ron the Milkman shot Ron the Italian.'

Rocky picked up the Bitch's leg. He dropped it. 'She's already stone cold.'

'She's been stone cold for years,' the Copper added.

They all laughed as if they were appearing in a badly written ITV comedy show.

After a struggle, four of them eventually lifted her up. Bob noticed an odd shaped instrument near her groin. 'What the hell is that?' he poked it.

'That's her strap-on.'

'Strap-on?'

'Yeah,' added the Sergeant, 'she always wore it...12 inch, it is...6-inch girth and bright black.'

'Oooohhhhhh,' moaned Rocky, 'bright black?'

'Blacker than the night, son, blacker than the night.'

They dragged her by her large feet down the stairs and out to the backyard. Down the years, many suspects had ended up in a gravelly grave after being beaten to death at the hands of the Plod. On the plus side, the tomatoes and cucumbers the Coppers had planted in the 6-metre squared section of grass, often won awards for their body and their earthy taste!

As the gang dug a Wicked Bitch shaped hole in the soft earth, the wizard walked passed holding a loaf of bread like a baby.

'Look what they did,' the priest stated, ignoring the fact there was a dead body next to a freshly dug grave, 'look, what they did to this poor defenceless baby. It's all mouldy.'

'Never mind that, Father Wizard...we've done it...we've got you all the funding you needed. Here.' She handed over the notepad. The wizard threw the bread over his left shoulder. It landed near Bob's feet. He booted it over the roof, 'one, nil.'

Father Wizard read the note. A small smile lifted up his mouth. 'Thank you...thank you...how can I ever repay you?'

Baglady marched forward, grabbing his arm. 'If it's not too much trouble, you can give me a fecking house to start with.'

'Ok...I did promise.' He rubbed his chin, 'Right....house...house.'

She folded her arms. 'Yeah, a proper one mind...inside toilet...conservatory...sauna, whirl pool.'

'You don't want much do you?' He shook his head. 'But unless someone gives us one...you will have to go on the waiting list.'

'How long is the waiting list?' She demanded, He unravelled a piece of paper with waiting list printed on the top. It touched the floor. 'Fine bloody wizard you are.'

The Wicked Bitch, lying out on the floor, started coughing. No one noticed her at first.

The priest continued. 'Unless we know someone who's just died with a big house?'

They all stood around scratching their heads. The Wicked Bitch coughed again and pointed to herself. Still no one took any notice. She got up onto her feet. Everyone had their backs to her. She pulled her keys out of her pocket and walked towards them.

'My house is now free.' She handed the keys to the Wizard.

'Fucking hell,' Bob gulped, 'She's a zombie...ARRGGGHHHHH.'

Rocky screamed. 'ZOMBIE...ZOMBIE.'

They all raced to the back door to try and get back into the Cop shop.

'Look,' the Wicked Bitch muttered, 'I've changed...I'm sorr...y...'

Dorothy whacked her full force over the head with a shovel. The woman's head exploded, sending blood, skin and brains over Dorothy's dress.

'Fucking hell, Dorothy,' the Baglady walked back out of the door, 'you are starting to give Fred West a fucking run for his money, love.'

'Hey...I have an idea,' the Wizard climbed out of the grave where he'd been hiding, and announced, 'why don't you have the Wicked Bitch's house?'

'Where is it?' asked Baglady suspiciously.

'Oh no, sorry,' he shook his head in disappointment, 'it's in the posh part of town.' Her eyebrows cocked up. 'Unless you can put up with all the school teachers and their swingers' parties?' he added.

'I'll give it a fucking go.' She skipped off like a teenage boy skipping home, sniffing his fingers, after getting to third base for the first time with his girlfriend.

The priest turned to Bob. 'Bob...Bob...Bob a Job. Look, it's a bad time for employment in the town. Factories are closing down, there are no coal mines anymore, but there is one job that's come up.' Bob gulped, 'but I'm not sure if you would like it or not.'

'Don't tell me it's a traffic warden...I hate traffic wardens.'

Baglady piped up, 'But you haven't got a car.'

'You don't need a car to hate fucking traffic wardens.'

Everyone nodded in agreement. Father Wizard gently coughed. 'Can I continue please? There're babies up on the estate getting turned into toasted sandwiches as we speak. Right there's a new company opening up in the retail park, it's called Drugs R Us and they are looking for someone who can roll an 8 skinner with one hand while scratching their nuts with the other. Is that any good?' Bob smiled. 'Oh, I'm not sure,' the priest added, Bob stopped smiling, 'they're only paying...3 grand...a week.'

Another smile, but this time much broader, attached itself to the ex-roadie's face like a two-day old rash. 'If I have 166 days holiday a year and 50% discount on staff sales? I'm your man...maaaaaaaaan.'

They shook hands on the deal.

'And now, you.' the priest faced Rocky, 'my overweight Billy Elliot...another hard one.'

'Ding bloody dong,' Rocky muttered, one hand on hip in true New York gay scene style.

The Wizard quickly moved back a couple of paces. 'I like your spirit but sadly there's no funding for anything like the arts around here anymore. The school kids couldn't even put a Christmas panto on. It's shocking.'

'Hang on,' Dorothy interrupted them. She walked towards the dead body of the Wicked Bitch. Talking to herself she scribbled some words on to a piece of paper. 'For being so short sighted and slashing the funding to all arts and development in the town...and giving no future to the kids, I'm so sorry. And to make up for it, here's a million pound...signed,' she picked up the Wicked Bitch's hand, 'the Wicked Bitch.'

'That's put a different egg in the basket' the priest said, 'this will give the old theatre in town the money to get refurbished and you, Rocky can be its creative director.'

'Yesssss,' Rocky clapped his hands. 'Ooooooh I'm so excited...I'm going to dance.'

The Wizard grabbed his arm and whispered, 'we'd rather if you fucking didn't.'

Everyone stood about patting each other on the back. The Wizard picked up the bread and began to walk away.

'Not so fast Billy Whizz,' yelled Bob, 'what about Dorothy?'

'Yes,' Baglady chipped in, 'how about Dorothy?'

'Don't worry about her,' the Wicked Bitch groaned, 'she's a mental case...lock her up.'

'Fuck me, she's still not dead....it easier to kill the Terminator,' said Bob.

'BBBBRRRRRRRRRRRRR,' Dorothy blasted her again with the machine gun. Everyone stared at the bullet riddled body of the once queen of Merthyr. Dorothy spun around, 'Oh, I don't think you can help me, Mister Wizard, I come from a long, way away.'

'Well, no...no...on the contrary. You have forced me into a cataclysmic decision. The only way to get Dorothy back to Bedlong is for me to take her there myself!'

A loud Oooohhhhhhh sound rose up from the watching crowd.

'Are you a clever enough Wizard to do that?' the girl asked.

Another loud Ooooohhhhhh.'

'If he says no,' a Copper muttered to Baglady, 'she will probably shoot his bollocks off.'

The priest glared at the officers before adding, 'Child...you cut me to the quick! I'm an old Bedlinog man myself...born and in-bred.' He took off one shoe to reveal a webbed foot with 8 toes and a thumb. He stood on the Wicked Bitch's dead body and turned to face everyone. 'Good people of Gurnoz, I, your Wizard par ardua ad alta, am about to embark upon a hazardous and technically unexplainable journey into the outer stratosphere.' He looked at the Copper at the front with a dumb expression on his ace. He talked in a thick Welsh accent, 'I'm going up the valley...where men are men and sheep are grateful. Come on Dorothy. '

Dorothy looked at the rest of her gang. 'Oh, it's...it's going to be so hard to say goodbye. I love you all, too.' She kissed the Baglady on the cheek.

'Get off me, you, big lesbo.'

'I'll come and visit you in your new house.'

'If you do...bring gin.'

Baglady gave her a hug back. A single tear rolled down the old woman's cheek.

She hugged Rocky. 'Go break a leg, Rocky.'

He leapt up on a wheelie bin but fell backwards onto the grass.

'For fuck sake,' Baglady hissed, 'he's like fucking Norman Wisdom.'

Rocky leapt back up onto his feet. 'It's not Rocky anymore...Its Rocky La Vue.'

'Way to go Rocky La Vue...way to go,' Dorothy shouted.

176

Next, the girl from Bedlinog tried to catch around Bob. 'I think I will miss you most of all Bob.'

'What?' he sat crossed legged on the floor. The biggest joint ever in his mouth.

'You...I will miss you most of all.'

'Where you going, en?'

Dorothy rolled her eyes. 'Stop smoking that bloody dope.'

'But it's my job now, mun.' He smirked and fell back onto the grass. He stared up at a crow eating the crust of a Gregg's pasties on a lamppost.

'Are you ready?' Father Wizard checked his watch, 'we haven't got all day.'

'Say goodbye, Terry.' Dorothy waved Terry's paw to everyone.

'Goodbye Terry,' everyone shouted back.

'Now close your eyes, and tap your heels together three times and say, there's no place like Bedlinog; there's no place like Bedlinog; there's no place like home.'

Dorothy took a deep breath. 'There's no place like Bedlinog.' Everyone stepped in closer. 'There's no place like Bedlinog.' You could hear a pin drop. 'There's no place like home.'

BANG!

A big ball of grey smoke covered the couple and the dog.

A woman screamed. 'Oh no....they blew up.' When the smoked cleared. Dorothy and the Wizard and Terry stood there. 'It's ok...they are still there,' the woman added, 'Fuck...someone stole my handbag.' A fight broke out.

Dorothy looked around and then at the man of the cloth. 'That didn't fuckin' work, did it?'

'I'm a priest not Paul fucking Daniels. How the hell did you think a pair of shoes was going to get you back home......TAXI!

Chapter 16

SHEEP IN RUBBER CLOTHING

While Dorothy, the Wizard and Terry travelled back to Bedlinog in an old, beaten up 60/60 cab, everyone else pissed off to the Gurnoz club where a load of drink, drugs and more drugs were consumed. During all the commotion that took place outside the cop shop, they forgot to bury the shot-up body of the Wicked Bitch. She lay near her makeshift grave, her lifeless eyes looking up towards the grey, rainy skies.

Hours later, when the darkness popped over the hill, a rustling could be heard in the bushes. From out of the shadows, a shadowy figure emerged. The gimp had been waiting a lifetime for this moment, this chance, and this opportunity.

On all fours and with the grace of a scalded cat, he headed towards the dead corpse on the ground. Under his mask, a huge grin lit up his normally dour face. The Viagra he had taken 20 minutes ago had kicked in. His small 4-inch penis like a throbbing pimple almost bursting out of his rubber gear.

He held his breath as he loomed over her. Sweat soaked his entire body. His heart beat in his chest like a lumberjack chopping wood. He poked her a few times to make sure she was actually dead. A slug crawled out of her ears. The gimp flicked it off her.

'She's all mine,' he grunted, while turning her over. He rubbed his hands, took the sharp scissors and a large tube of KY jelly out of his pocket and went in for the kill!!!!

Chapter 17

NICE DAY FOR A MAD WEDDING

It was the greatest wedding Bedlinog had ever witnessed. Freaks, weirdos, nuts and hairy people from every corner of the Valley turned up to celebrate. Thousands waited impatiently outside the small cow shed *(which you may remember not only doubled up as a delivery room (chapter 1), but also trebled up as a church, plus a betting office, laundrette and also held belly dancing classes every Wednesday evening from 6 until 9).*

People cheered when the couple slowly marched out of the church (cow shed) doors. People cried, when a two headed biker toasted the bride. Children threw dead budgies at the couple. Apparently an old Bedlinog tradition (probably started by the bloke who owned the pet shop and couldn't sell live budgies in the first place.)

Dorothy looked radiant in her white wedding dress, holding a bunch of flowers. Dozy Git's smile was so wide it wrapped itself around the cow shed several times over.

'There's no place like Bedlinog, Dozy Git.'

'Me's luvs you...Mrs Dozy Git.'

'And me luvs you too, Mister Dozy Git.'

Dozy Git swung his foot as if kicking a football in the last minute of the FA Cup final. 'Back of the fucking net,' He put his shirt over his head to reveal his five nipples and a tap where his belly button should have been.

As the speakers blasted out the music of Shakin' Steven's Green Door, the newlyweds disappeared into their new home to consummate the marriage. Everyone else went over to Uncle Henry's and Aunty Em's shed and got pissed on something that looked like gin but tasted like petrol. Hours later, in a drunken haze, most of the wedding guests ended up in one giant, satanic orgy. A great day was had by all.

The day after, Terry the dog went looking for love in Brighton or it could have been Belgium!

Chapter 18

WHERE IS THEY ALL NOW?

Although they never had any kids, **Dorothy and Dozy Git** lived a blissful life in Bedlinog for a few years, until she discovered that her husband was having an affair with the devil goat with the bent penis which had a bell-end that looked like Alan Shearer. They got divorced soon after. Dorothy still wears her white stilettoes every day and cries most nights.

Terry the dog did move to Brighton, not Belgium. With the sparkle of bright lights and cheap drugs, he got heavily involved in the doggy gay scene. Recently, he got married to Butch, a big, black bullmastiff. They are in the process of adopting their first pup, a small Shih Tzu

Baglady still lives in luxury in the Wicked Bitch's house in the posh part of town. Just for kicks, every night she shits in her neighbour's garden. They know it is her, but they are too afraid to say anything.

Bob went back roadying for a short while with Irish super group, U2. But as expected, he got sacked after losing Bono's famous glasses and then for drawing a penis on the Edge's bald head when he was fast asleep on the tour bus.

Rocky's first ever stage play, *A Welsh Side Story,* telling the violent, love story of two Merthyr gangs, the Swansea Roaders and the Gurnoz shop gang, battling it out for world domination, is due to open in Broadway, sorry, Broadmoor, in the summer of 2020.

Glinda still works in Hing Hongs even though it closed 15 years ago. Secretly she dreams of becoming a nun and climbing Everest in flip flops while carrying a plate of fried rice with a fried egg on the top. She's already started training.

The Gimp was sacked from his gimping job in the council after the death of his master. He now works in Debenhams up on the Retail Park on the make-up counter. He's won Employee of the Month for the last six months on the tamp.

Thug Boy is due to appear on Love Island in 2023 if he gets out of prison for good behaviour.

Sidekick and the rest of the gang formed a Temptation Tribute Band but they split after a few gigs because they couldn't sing, were a little too white and they didn't know the Temptations had never worn purple and white shell suits.

Billy Wizard, the priest, disappeared in a puff of smoke one night after drinking three bottles of red wine in a cool bar in Swansea. Rumour has it that he's a dolphin trainer working in the South of France.

The Mayor and his wife were both arrested and imprisoned for two years after graphic and very explicit photos of ex-mayors and their wives were discovered on their computer.

Aunty Em and Uncle Henry still make special chicken feed and recently won the biggest omelette in the world competition in Bala in North Wales. To celebrate, they held a two-week, non-stop orgy in their barn. Free condoms, KY gel and poppers were available to all guests.

The Ghost of the Wicked Bitch was often seen posing on a wall in the middle of town pretending to be the famous statue she always craved. Last week, a youth sneaked up on her and stuck a traffic cone on her head and wrote Twwat on her forehead in black marker. She hasn't been seen since.

Merthyr Town is one day hoping to become the city of culture, once it builds a cathedral, a few more kebab shops and fully understands what the word culture means.

THE END
(or is it?)

A few words of thank to some very special people: -

The play, which this book is loosely based on, would never have been written without my good mate, **Paul O Sullivan** sitting in my garden, drinking red wine and telling each other stories of weird stuff.

Next, is **Neil Maidman**, the director of the original play, the wizard of gurnwah, who took our ramblings and moulded them into a first-class stage production which had people rolling in the aisles and numerous injunctions taking out against us.

The cast of the wizard of gurnwah (too many to name) who added their own bit of sugar and spice to the original play and helped develop the character into actual people who now live and breathe inside my head every day.

The people of my rough, old, tough, old town who have supported and encouraged Gurnwah Productions for the last few years.

Marc Phillips for the brilliant cover design and putting up with me being a right pain in the arse.

Joe Strummer of The Clash for lighting up my life

The serious bit: -

Merthyr and Valleys Mind. - ItTakesBallstotalk.

I decided to give all money made from this novel to the charitable organisation – Merthyr and Valleys Minds and their new campaign, ItTakesBallstotalk. Over the last few years, there have been some tragic events in my town where people have taken their own lives due to depression and mental health issues.

I grew up in a "man's world" environment, where things like depression and anxiety were laughed upon and often dismissed with a joke or a comment like "shut up, you nutter, get another drink down you."

I just think now, it is time for us all to be more aware of the danger signs and try our best to help and / or get professional help for these individuals.

I would like to thank the following people / businesses for covering the publishing costs so that any money received will now go straight to the charity. In no particular order: -

- Keith Power
- RA Bush
- Neil Maidman
- Colour House
- Paul Trotman
- Mazo
- Kerry Jones – K. Jones – scrap metal, recycling & demolition
- Steve Sims – Creative Signs Wales Ltd
- Mike Wiskey Driscoll – QC Partnership Ltd
- Alex Thomas and Wiskey - White Horse
- Merthyr Rising/ Redstone Productions
- Jonny Owen – writer / director – (To the Real Mayor of Merthyr...my great friend, Anthony Bunko. Always happy to help...Jonny X)

See below for more details if you want to donate or buy the book:-

So, if you would like to help...there are two possible next steps:

1. If you are a local business / group / individual and would like to donate anything towards this then please click on the link below.

2. If you would like to buy a signed copy (retailing at £6.99 but if you want a tenner would mean more money in the pot) then please go to www.gurnwah.co.uk and click on the link to pre - order it now.

Books will be available to pick up or purchase direct at the book shop at Theatr Soar or the Merthyr and Valleys MIND office in the high street in Merthyr. Or go to this website and follow the link

https://gurnwah.co.uk

Stay Free

Bunko xx